CONTROLLED
LOVING AN ALPHA MALE

S.K. LESSLY

JESSICA WATKINS PRESENTS

SYNOPSIS

Control: the power to influence or direct people's behavior or the course of events. It is indicative to such words as power, command, dominance, and leadership.

Hello,

Let me introduce myself. My name is Andrew Pierce, known to everyone as A.P. I'm a corporate attorney on the fast-track to becoming partner at the Law Firm of Goldstein, Parker, & Foster. My tamed hair is blonde, and my eyes are blue. I stand above six feet with pure muscle covering my entire body. I exude confidence, strength, aggressiveness, power and most of all, control. Shit, if I'm to be honest here… I am the *epitome* of fucking control.

Most people strive to have control, but they don't know the first thing about it. They use it as a means to harm, destroy or dominate. For me, control is like breathing. It's my lifeline. I must have control. I must be *in* control. It's not about my sick twisted need to dominate that's ingrained in me no matter what. No, control for me is simple, it's a matter of life or death.

I've worked all of my life to master the art of control and believe me, it wasn't easy. I have been tested, measured, and judged, but I never allow myself to succumb to the loss of control. So imagine my damn surprise, my panic, when for the first time in forever my control falters. Shit, it happened so fast that I couldn't stop it. My breathing became erratic, and my heart beat raced so fast that I wasn't sure if I would be able to… *control* it.

I thought this was it, and I looked around my surroundings, frantically looking for the source of my lapse, waiting to destroy the threat, when my eyes fell on…*heaven*. This beautiful, stunning, magnificent woman before me stole my breath away. She was the reason why my control faltered. This was dangerous for a man like me, losing control like this. I knew what I must do; however, I still couldn't move. It was that moment when I realized that for the first time in my life, I was fucked.

Copyright © 2016 by S.K. Lessly
Published by Jessica Watkins Presents

All rights reserved, including the right of reproduction in whole or in part in any form. Without limiting the right under copyright reserved above, no part of this publication may be reproduced, stored in or introduced into a retrieval system, or transmitted, in any form by means (electronic, mechanical, photocopying, recording, or otherwise), without the prior written permission of the copyright owner.

This is a work of fiction. Names, characters, places and incidents are either the product of the author's imagination or are used fictitiously, and any resemblance to actual persons, living or dead, business establishments, events, or locales, is entirely coincidental.

❦ Created with Vellum

PROLOGUE

He felt her familiar warm and gentle touch flow through his golden, thick locks. It traveled along his scalp, sending a sensation that started from the tips of her fingers down through every nerve ending in his body. He then felt her soft lips. They lightly touched his right temple, then his ear, sending his senses into hyper drive. A whisper suddenly tickled the side of his face, pleading for him to come out of the darkness. The hypnotic scent of her essence brought him the much needed peace as his brain registered the familiarity of her voice. As he felt the haze that held him captive slowly dissipate, it was then that he felt the limp body underneath him.

Rough hands grabbed him under his arms and drug him until the smell of freshly cut grass overwhelmed him. A knee to his back branded him to the cold earth, but he didn't fight. It was as if his body was detached from his brain. He couldn't register what was happening to him. The unexpected cold metallic feel of steel against his heated skin released more of the deadly haze he was in, enough for him to focus on the lifeless body before him.

What the hell is going on? he asked himself.

He couldn't remember shit.

He didn't understand what was happening or why it was happening. Did he know the man lying before him? The man's lifeless body- a victim of someone's wrath- laid there unmoving, his chest barely expanding. He couldn't see the man's face; it was covered in blood.

He sucked his teeth. *Whoever fucked him up was pissed as hell.*

His thoughts and the sound of a woman's insistent pleas were keys to unlocking his prison, everything flooded back to him, including why he was there. "Let him go! He didn't do anything wrong! He was protecting me, protecting himself. You have to believe me! Please, God! You're wasting time! Please!"

He felt his body go ridged and his instincts kicked in as the cries he heard brought him completely into the light. Her words finally hit its mark, piercing him through his rage-induced haze.

He could feel her fear, her anguish, and it was ripping into him. He struggled to take in a breath as a soft whisper finally labored through his lips. "Nyla…"

MONTHS EARLIER...

CHAPTER 1

"Nyla, your boyfriend is here," Dee Dee called out as she peeked out of the heavy revolving kitchen doors.

Nyla, who had just emerged from the walk-in refrigerator in the back of the kitchen, looked in the direction of the front of Rocky's Diner. With her hands full of produce, Nyla couldn't help the smile that creased her face as she thought about "her boyfriend."

Well, he really isn't my boyfriend, she corrected herself.

He was, however, the biggest crush she had ever had in her life; the star of every fantasy she had since he first arrived about a month ago.

"Is he by himself? How does he look?" she asked her friend and fellow waitress with a slight quiver in her voice.

Dee Dee laughed. "Girl, you know I don't go that way. I like my meat dark, as well as my men, but I will say he's kinda hot for a white guy."

Nyla looked at Dee Dee and shook her head. Diane "Dee Dee" Church and Nyla grew up as different as night and day. Dee Dee was pale with black hair that hung to the middle of her back. She grew up in the less than favorable part of the city with drugs and gangs all around her. She was tough, with street smarts embedded in her, as well as the skills to stay alive in the war zone that was her neighborhood. Nyla Montgomery, on the other hand, was born and raised in the suburbs of the city. Her complexion was brown, and her black hair was shortly worn in a signature pixie style, tapered on the sides and back and extra-long on the top, tumbling over her forehead. Nyla had never fought for anything in her life but maintaining good grades. She didn't have a preference in the men she dated; she only preferred that they weren't assholes. She had never experienced the tough choices that life presented others, but she was getting a crash course as of late.

"Is he by himself?" Nyla asked Dee Dee again.

Dee Dee suddenly frowned and shook her head. "Ah, no, suga. Sorry, he's with Snow White."

The smile that had creased Nyla's face a moment earlier suddenly died. She placed the produce down on the kitchen counter next to Rock and moved to the door of the kitchen. She took a few deep breaths to gather herself before she stepped from behind the doors. She always hesitated before she headed toward him. It was the time she needed to remind herself that he would never be hers—he belonged to someone else.

That "someone else" happened to be the woman that had been accompanying him to the diner for weeks. "Snow White" was what Dee Dee started calling her the moment they saw her. She was almost perfect in Nyla's eyes. Her black hair was perfectly combed, her skin was perfectly tanned, and her looks were as all else, perfect. The only thing keeping Snow White from complete perfection was the disgusted look on her face that was always present the moment they walked into the diner.

Nyla hated Snow White and everything she stood for. Nyla believed that women like Snow White did everything that they could to tear down women like herself; putting their status in everyone's faces, feeling as though their *privilege* gave them the right of passage and everyone around them should feel fortunate just to be in their presence. She also represented everything Nyla wasn't; the kind of woman that had no problem getting and keeping the kind of man that sat across from her. There was one thing that Nyla would love to thank her for, however; she'd heard her say his name...A.P.

A.P.

She didn't have a clue what the initials stood for, but she felt that knowing his name seemed to bring them closer together. She'd quietly learned so much about him by just watching him. She noticed the little things, like how deep his clean-shaven handsome face frowned when he got frustrated, how his eyes grew a dark shade of blue when he was angry. The sound of a man's voice was something Nyla never thought would get her hot and bothered, but the sound of *his* voice, that authoritative way he asked for his omelet, always made her insides grow moist.

Anything she could find to bring her close to him, she paid attention to. She knew nothing about who he was, where he lived, or what he did for a living. Right now, her attraction was purely physical, from his broad chest, to his large hands and long fingers, to his square chin, and striking blue eyes. She was in awe of him. His lips were so inviting and sensual that no matter what she tried to do, she couldn't keep her eyes off them. She wondered how they would feel against her neck and against her own lips.

The woman he was with didn't deserve him. Nyla not only knew this, but she felt it. The woman was superficial and Nyla knew that wasn't what A.P. deserved. He deserved to be cherished and desired beyond measure. He deserved to be taken care of, held, and touched in all the right places.

She shook her head and closed her eyes.

Get off of fantasyland, Nyla, she berated herself. *There's no way he will ever fall for a woman like you.*

No matter how much she longed for him, she felt in her heart that she just wasn't his type.

When she emerged from the kitchen and her eyes settled on him, she smiled.

Damn, he is so good looking.

Today A.P. wore a simple, dark navy suit with a crisp white shirt and no tie. His shirt was open at the top, and she could just make out his tamed chest hairs. Her heart started to beat out of control. Nyla leaned on the counter and just watched him. How he sat erect in his chair reading his newspaper- *Who does that anymore?* His wavy, blonde hair sat neatly in place. His cologne filled the dining room and drove her crazy. But, the moment *she* spoke to him and he looked up at her, giving this woman all of his attention, the daydream died for Nyla. Nyla was forced to swallow the bitter taste of reality as she made her way to the table.

He could never be hers.

ANDREW PIERCE, or A.P. to everyone he knew, had sensed her presence before she emerged from the back of the diner. It continued to amaze him how much she affected him, and how he could sense her without seeing her. What he felt would sometimes seep profoundly into his core, overwhelming him, and it began one morning some weeks ago when he first walked into Rock's Diner. That particular morning, Andrew was in search of a place that sold great coffee, somewhere other than the overpriced coffee chain, Starbucks. He remembered overhearing someone from his office mentioning a diner that sat on Peco and Dressler that opened early in the morning and sold great coffee, which was fresh all the time. When he pulled his Black Infinity Q50S into the parking lot at 7am, he started not to get out. He loved his coffee but shit, he didn't want to smell like grease for the entire day. The place looked as if someone used a time machine to travel back to the fifties, extricated the popular diner into their small remote town with only two-hundred people, and settled it here. It looked so authentic from the outside and completely out of place for this artsy neighborhood, but looking in the window, the place seemed packed.

"Okay, just go in quickly, ask for a cup to go, and get out," he coached himself.

He unfolded himself out of his car and headed for the steps of the diner. When he opened the door to Rock's Diner and stepped inside, just as he thought, he felt his arteries clog up from the sheer smell of grease. He hadn't had anything fried in years, and as his heart became constricted by just the smell of the heavily greased foods, he knew he needed to continue that healthy habit.

Stay the course A.P., he encouraged himself.

He looked around the diner and smirked. It was as he noticed from the outside; packed. This place was as authentic inside as it was outside. The booths and tables were the authentic diner-style, straight from the fifties with vinyl-covered benches and chairs. There was a bar-style counter stretching just about the length of the place with bolted down rounded vinyl-covered stools, situated underneath the counter. The tables that were strategically placed around the room had chairs with chrome legs and chrome strips, which accented both the tables and the front counter.

Regardless of the aged look and seemingly caked on grease that looked to cover the walls and windows of this place, no one seemed to care.

As Andrew surveyed the room, he noticed that the breakfast counter that stretched the length of the diner seemed to be the place to go to be in and out. He looked at his watch. He had a meeting in about forty-five minutes.

I can make it if I...

The rest of Andrew's thoughts suddenly fell away as a familiar feeling unexpectedly came over him. It was something that he hadn't felt in years. No, he was wrong. What he now felt was nothing he had ever felt before in his life. He quickly searched his surroundings, looking for a source of this sudden surge of emotion, wishing for the impossible, when his eyes fell on her. His heart seemingly stopped in mid-beat. He gripped the door handle next to him, trying his best to get a hold of the visceral urges that were suddenly threatening to take over. Could she be the reason he was feeling this way?

The sensation that was overpowering him was becoming too much for him. He could feel the aggression in his eyes, burning him to his core. He closed them quickly.

Fuck, this can't be happening. Not here!

It wasn't until he felt a profound and dominant rumble building within the pits of his soul that he realized just how out of control he was getting. Something was pulling his inner being out; it was calling to him, taunting him, pushing him. Fuck, he was beginning to slip back into complete darkness, something that he hadn't done in a very long time.

A growl that suddenly fell from his lips tumbled him back into the light. He removed his hand from the dented door handle behind him. He hadn't felt like this since…

His breath hitched in his throat, at the implication of what he was thinking, as he blinked a few times, trying desperately to gather himself. She was the cause of what was happening to him, which was clear. He was being pulled toward her; with a salacious and dominating force so strong, it rendered him helpless.

He attempted to look away from her, hoping that his heart would start to beat, that the blood would stop pulsing frantically in his ears, and that the sudden urge to claim this woman would subside, but neither happened. He was battling the engrained desire to claim her right here in this diner.

Fuck, he couldn't breathe.

His heart had been comfortably on ice for a very long time, and he had not intended for it to thaw. He rather liked feeling that way. It worked for him in the courtroom, in the office and since he was a cold-hearted asshole, he had been able to be by himself without reproach. However, as he watched her move around the diner, speaking to a few customers as she glided, he felt his heart warm a bit.

This cannot be happening!

He was just about to turn around and leave before he found himself relinquished of all self-control when her eyes finally met his. He held her there, unable to take his eyes from her sweet, hazel ones. She was undeniably beautiful. Her skin was the color of the Dove chocolate nuggets that he kept in his desk drawer at work and at home. She radiated through the grime and dismal weight of this place, bringing about peace and welcoming so strong that he wondered if it was her that had this place filled with people, rather than the food.

She was graceful, with just the simple things that she did, such as walking, waving or just taking someone's order. He was stunned at how much she exuded life and a tenderness that captivated everyone around her with just her smile. He could see how rich and deep her eyes were without even being close. She was exotic to him, with high cheekbones and a bow tie shaped mouth that made him daydream about how they would look wrapped around him, touching him.

He felt his face frown slightly; confusion laced his mind as he tried to figure out why she was invoking these feelings from him, why he couldn't stop looking at her, why he wanted desperately to have her. He felt like he was under some type of spell.

Disbelief choked him swiftly.

No, this can't be what I think it is, he tried to convince himself. *Could it?*

Could what he'd been told all those years ago be true?

Before he could admit to himself the possibilities, she broke the spell between them.

Get yourself together, Pierce, he coached himself as he pulled a deep breath into his lungs, doing his best to treat this moment as any other encounter he had with a human being.

Wait a minute. Is that a hint of chocolate I smell? Shit...

The waitress came closer to him and eyed him cautiously. Andrew placed his hands in his pants pockets just to have something to do with them, as he greeted her. "Coffee to go, black, two sugars, no cream."

She seemed startled slightly by his tone and stepped back from him.

Shit! he repeated in his mind while figuratively kicking his own ass.

He knew his bluntness could be construed as him being a heartless bastard. He had to fix it quickly before she walked away or, by the frown that developed on her angelic face, cussed his ass out.

He placed his hands up quickly. "I apologize for my abruptness."

Wait, what? His eyebrows shot up in disbelief. He'd never apologized for shit he said or did and yet here he was....

Andrew moved closer to her, willing her not to turn and run from him. "Let me try that again. I would really appreciate it if I could have a cup of coffee to go. My morning has gone to shit already because I left the house without getting my fix. Please have pity on me and accept my apology."

He felt the side of his mouth curl, a motion that his mouth rarely did, and held his breath.

The waitress studied him before she smiled shyly saying, "I guess I can understand that."

Ho-ly fuck! Her voice.

"So, am I forgiven for my rudeness?" he prodded, realizing he was still holding his breath, his anticipation becoming too much...

This is bullshit!

In that moment, her smile brightened before his eyes. She then tilted her head slightly and shyly looked up at him.

"Yes, you're forgiven."

Andrew found himself studying her again. He couldn't help it. He watched the innocence, the vulnerability, and the longing convey through her eyes. He could see right through to her soul; she was so open. Her sweetness was just a touch away; he saw and sensed that she had no clue how sexy or how beautiful she was. That thought alone not only made his dick hard as a boulder but also made him want her even more.

Realizing that he had been standing before her, watching her for too damn long, he cleared his throat.

"Thanks," was the only reply he managed to get out of his garbled mind.

He'd never been at a loss for words. However, standing in front of this woman, all he could think about was taking her body on every table, every chair and wall of this place, grease and all. He wanted her smiles to be his. He wanted her touch and her taste to belong to him. He wanted to claim her, dominate her in every pleasurable way. He wanted to hear her cry out his name in ecstasy, feel her pussy tighten along his dick, feel her grip his back as he lost control and pounded into her relentlessly over and over and...

"Shit," he drawled out silently as he ran his hand through his hair.

What was she doing to him?

The remarkable smile that quickly emerged along her features managed to make his dick threaten to bust through the front of his slacks and claim her itself. He shoved his hands back inside of his pants pockets to make sure she didn't see just how she was affecting him physically. He couldn't stop what she was doing to him, and if he was honest with himself, he didn't want to either.

The waitress, oblivious to what was happening before her spoke softly, "Okay, well if you wish to have a seat at the counter behind me, I'll get you what you're craving for."

Andrew nodded his reply and watched as she turned to head for the coffee machine behind the counter. The hunger that he had for this waitress was something that he wouldn't be able to ignore. This was going to be new territory for him. He had never dated outside of his race, but that didn't bother him. He didn't care about the color of any woman's skin; he cared about what made them special. He cared about having that life-altering connection shared between two people.

There had been one woman in his life that he felt he had a special connection with. They were together for three years, until one day they weren't. Her departure was sudden, which left him bitter, closed off and empty. He believed he would never have that type of connection with another woman. Yet, here he was, never wanting this penetrating yearning for this chocolate goddess to go away. What he needed to do, however, was to get a hold of his growing desires to possess her. He must tread lightly. In no way could he fuck this up. His soul had to have her.

Without fucking question...She. Was. His.

CHAPTER 2

"Are we really going to keep coming here?" Lori asked him, bringing him back to the present.

He was pretending to be engrossed in his newspaper, looking at stock numbers he had already reviewed on his iPad before he left his condo. It was rudimentary he knew, but he had to do something to take his mind off of Nyla.

Without looking up at Lori, he replied, "You didn't have to come, Lori; I tell you this every morning, but still you make it a point to meet me here."

"Well, unfortunately, this seems to be the only place I get to see you *and* talk to you outside of your office," she retorted quickly. "Besides, I'm hoping that you'll quickly satisfy your slumming *need* and stop coming here altogether."

Finally, he moved his eyes from the tiny print and placed them on her.

"Lori, no one's keeping you here. It's obvious, you've satisfied your *own* need. I've been seen and we've talked. You can put yourself out of your own misery and leave knowing that you've accomplished what you set out to do."

"Well, actually, I haven't accomplished what I set out to do. I haven't experienced the full force of your winning personality so I can get through my mundane existence. So, I think I'll stick around and-"

Andrew's focus habitually shifted from the ramblings of the blonde sitting across from him to the familiar impatience of waiting. He was just about to turn and look for *her* when suddenly, as if on cue, his heart rate started rapidly beating against its cage.

Oh, yes, there she is.

He closed his eyes and consumed her being as she stood watching him. He knew she was watching him. Not only did he feel it but he also sensed it; her craving for him, her longing. Instead of reacting to her arrival, he brought his distorted focus back to his paper.

Concentrate, damn it, he told himself.

He felt her come closer to his table, keeping her heavenly honey eyes on him the whole way, he knew. She placed a coffee cup in front of him and as she poured, she said smiling, "Good morning."

"Good morning," he replied in his usual clipped tone. *Why are you such an asshole?* It wasn't on purpose he knew, however he'd been this way for so long, he didn't have a clue how to be different.

"Are you going to have your usual?" she asked him, ignoring his bluntness. Hell, she was too busying trying not to notice the moistness that he produced in her by just being close.

"Yes, and can you tell the cook to sauté the mushrooms a little longer this time?" Andrew turned the page of the paper as nonchalantly as he could, keeping his eyes on the small meaningless black and white print.

"Yes, of course. Anything for you, miss?"

He glanced at Lori and groaned inwardly as she produced a placid smile that typically provided a false sense of pleasantness to anyone it was directed to. Unfortunately for Lori's victims, they didn't realize her true colors until it was too late.

"Yes," Lori said as Nyla greeted Lori's smile with one of her own. "Can you please bring me fuel and a match so I can light this hideous place on fire; putting everyone in here out of their misery?"

Andrew sighed and gave Lori a reproachful look. "Don't be a bitch, Lori."

He then shifted his eyes back to the useless paper and added absently, "Don't worry about her, Nyla; she's just here to be a reminder that birth control was a breakthrough in medical science and should be used all the time."

He heard Lori suck her teeth; the likely response from her. Who remained quiet was Nyla. He didn't hear a sound from her, nor did he see her move from his peripheral. Shit, he knew that sometimes his humor could be cruel and offensive. People that knew him expected some crass or harsh words from him, but Nyla didn't know him. He's behaved for weeks, not showing the bastard side of him too early and here he almost blew it.

What also bothered him was the length of the silence, so he risked looking at her and found her eyes were wide as saucers. It was then that he realized what he had done. It wasn't the sarcastic joke he told; it was the fact that he used her name.

Fuck.

They didn't wear nametags in this place, so there was no way he could justify knowing her name. He had actually drilled one of the bus boys that he caught outside of the diner one day about her. He didn't learn much about her but her name, which was enough for him.

Andrew shifted in his seat, thinking he would have a lot of explaining to do and was getting ready to change the subject when, in a blink of an eye, she changed. She started to shake slightly, which he caught instantly, and fear seeped through her pores like an alcoholic would reek of his favorite elixir.

What the hell? he wondered silently.

Andrew followed her eyes to two men that stood in the doorway of the diner, both he recognized and both were looking over at Nyla.

"Um, your order will be right up. If you will excuse me," she said, not looking in his direction, and moved quickly to the kitchen.

Andrew watched her disappear, then focused his eyes on the two men that had caused Nyla to scuttle away in fear—Robert Downs and

John Michaels. Downs was a millionaire twice over, who was born and raised in the area. He and his family were very successful in the commercial property industry and owned quite a few business properties in the city. The Downs' were the celebrities in the town, gaining respect and influence throughout the city. Andrew believed that Robert, however, gained his stardom by riding on his father's coattail.

Robert didn't do anything that would warrant his success or wealth. Robert's power was only present because of his last name. He believed people cowered to him and gave him what he wanted because of who he was. Robert Downs felt everyone owed him everything, and he owed nothing.

Andrew hated the son of a bitch. He was well aware of what Downs was made up of and knew his reason for being here couldn't be good for Nyla.

Nyla emerged from the back of the diner with her apron removed. She passed Andrew, chewing on her lower lip, twisting her trembling hands, seemingly concentrating on putting one foot in front of her. She met the two men at the door and led them to a booth on the other side of the diner. The trio sat down; Robert sitting on one side of the table, Nyla on the other, and Michaels sitting between them, bringing up a chair from another table.

Andrew tried not to stare, but he couldn't help it. He wondered what the hell Michaels was up to. John Michaels was the king of slime and evil. He was a corporate attorney to all of the spawns of satan that lived in the city. He was known to have only the elite as his clientele. Andrew knew that Michaels being there couldn't be good either, and seeing the uneasiness in Nyla's eyes told him that his suspicions were accurate. He also wondered what Robert had to do with Nyla. Downs would never bring himself to come on this side of town, much less in this diner to socialize.

He kept his eyes on the three, and even though they spoke in hush tones, he could see that Nyla was clearly affected by the presence of both of these men.

Another waitress came by his table and placed his omelet in front of him. He mumbled an incoherent, "Thank you," and absently started eating, never moving his eyes from across the room.

"God, Andrew, can you please hurry up so we can get out of here," Lori complained, but again Andrew ignored her.

As always, his focus was on one person, and, seeing the distress on her face and the sneaky slick way Michaels was leaning into her, he could tell something wasn't right. He could sense it. A slow, uncontrollable rumble permeated deep within him. It grew in strength and volume in his throat, and he didn't stop it, not when it grew deeper and not when it slowly escaped his mouth.

The sudden fear that arrested Lori's body also didn't stop Andrew from letting his true being take over. Nyla needed him. Everything in the diner fell away, leaving only Andrew, Nyla, Michaels and Downs. Andrew then noticed Nyla's facial expression change from the simple look of nervousness and trepidation to total panic and fear. She shook her head back and forth fervently and buried her face in her hands.

That's when Andrew had enough and moved quickly in her direction. When he got close, he saw Michaels push a document over and a pen.

"Trust me; this will be better for all parties," Andrew heard him say, as he smiled, smooth as the snake he was. "It's very simple and once you sign, this nightmare of a situation will go away. However, if you don't, this deal will never come a- Hey, what the-"

Michaels' eyes widened at the sight of Andrew as he snatched the paper from under Michaels' grip and started reading. Andrew said quickly, sliding next to Nyla, "I know you're not speaking to my client without me being present, Michaels?"

He felt Nyla's eyes on him, but he kept his eyes on the paper in his hand.

"What's the meaning of this?" he heard Robert boom. "Nyla, you fucking stupid whore. Didn't I tell you...?"

Andrew's head shot up sharply, eyes narrowed, and anger drenched in them. "Call her a whore again and you'll be eating my fist and this bullshit ass motion for breakfast."

Robert frowned, but he didn't say another word. Andrew then put the paper down, grabbed Nyla's hand and stood.

"This meeting is over."

"Wait. No, please," Nyla said to him, trying to move her hand from his, but Andrew didn't let go.

Andrew directed his attention to Michaels. "I can't believe you came here with this bullshit. You're really asking my client to give up her rights to this self-righteous son of a bitch? Get out of my sight with this now, before I rip this immoral and unlawful shit and shove it down both your throats."

Michaels shook his head and stood, not quite meeting Andrew eye-to-eye. "Pierce, you always manage to stick your nose in matters that don't concern you. I know for a fact she doesn't have a lawyer."

"Yes, she does. She retained me about an hour ago. I was trying to enjoy my meal before I came over here, but, apparently, you either didn't wait for my client to inform you that she had representation or you never asked, which I have to call into question any other paperwork you had her sign in the past."

Michaels looked down at Nyla and smiled, void of all emotion. "Clearly, this is bullshit. And let me remind you what we discussed before. You could lose big time if you-"

Andrew's expression viciously darkened even more, causing Michaels' words to fall away swiftly. Andrew moved closer to Michaels, pulled Nyla to her feet, and protectively shifted her behind him. Andrew shifted his eyes to Robert, then back to Michaels, never easing the intensity and anger from them.

"Understand, gentlemen, that from this day forward, you will not speak to my client again, do you understand? Try and bully her, and it will not end well, I assure you. I'm giving you the benefit of the doubt now, but this is my first and last warning." He again moved his eyes between both men before saying, "You don't want to test me."

Robert, trying to salvage what little dignity he had left, retorted, "You'll be sorry you ever stuck your nose in my business, Pierce. Do you have any idea who I am and who my father is? I'll have your job, your license-"

Andrew laughed interrupting Robert's rant. Andrew shook his head.

"It's apparent you don't have a clue who you're dealing with, so let me re-introduce myself." He reached inside of his suit jacket and pulled out his card. He placed it on the table in front of Robert, but spoke to both men.

"My name is Andrew Pierce. I have no conscience, and I have no fucking problem burying you without a second thought. So if you think of coming after me, make sure you come for me with everything you have. Because *I will* come after you with everything *I* have and more. I will embarrass you, take you for everything you have and leave you with nothing, not even the clothes on your fucking back. By the time I'm done with you, you won't know what end is up. Come after Ms. Montgomery and her daughter, and my words will be the least of your problems."

Michaels' eyebrows furrowed as his eyes moved from Nyla back to Andrew. Andrew met his gaze unwavering. He knew he could be very intimidating with just his steely gaze, but on this occasion, he used his size, eyes and aggression to bring home the point that he was no one to fuck with.

Jaws clenched, eyes cold, hard and flinty, Andrew bit coolly, "I expect to hear from you soon."

"You don't know what you're getting into, Pierce," Michaels reiterated slowly.

Andrew chortled, humor nonexistent, "Oh, but I do. The question you should ask yourself is why I'm so confident, besides the fact that I'm arrogant and a certified son of a bitch."

Michaels' demeanor suddenly went on heightened alert. He was very familiar with Andrew Pierce's reputation. Pierce was one of the best attorneys in the state. "The Hatchet" was what they called him and he lived up to that name ten times over. Pierce *was* an arrogant, son of a bitch that rarely played by the rules. He was as ruthless as they came. There were times Pierce made decisions to destroy companies in ways even he never thought of and Michaels knew he could be as cold and callous as Hitler himself. He had also seen Pierce show leniency in the past, something that Michaels, himself, didn't believe in. Michaels wasn't a slouch himself; he was one of the best too. He was acquired by the filthy-rich and successful because they knew *he* was the best. Michaels protected them. It was his calling to do so. He had a certain set of skills, manipulation and backstabbing, and used anyone he could to get to the top and helped other people in his status to do the same.

But Michaels wasn't stupid either. He needed to regroup.

Michaels stared at Andrew for a long moment before he backed away and signaled to Robert that they were leaving.

"Okay, Pierce," Michaels began. "We'll play this your way. I expect to have the proper paperwork, along with Ms. Montgomery's proposal, on my desk in a day or two."

Andrew moved closer to him, lips tightened with suppressed wrath. "No, *you* will contact my office in a day or two and my assistant will put you and that son of a bitch on my schedule whenever I have the fucking time. Then we will sit down and we will discuss what's best for that little girl, understand?" Andrew then lowered his voice for only Robert and Michaels to hear and warned, "My advice… Don't leave here and try to grow a set of balls; that's the last thing you want to do. Goodbye, gentlemen."

Andrew left the two standing by the booth and moved purposefully between the tables around him, taking a hesitant and visibly shaken Nyla with him. He weaved his way through the curious patrons, passed a confused Lori and moved to the back of the kitchen.

"Hey, you can't-," Rock started to say, but stopped instantly when he saw that Andrew was with Nyla.

Andrew turned to a frowning Nyla as she snatched her hand from his.

"Do you have any idea what you've done?" she asked through clenched teeth, eyes narrowed and nose flared.

Andrew, unexpectedly turned on, tried not to smile at her. The anger and aggression that was rolling off her in that moment made her undeniably stunning to him.

Nyla smacked his arm. "Answer me, damn it."

Andrew took a deep breath and said to her, "Yes, of course, I know exactly what I've done. You're welcome, by the way."

Nyla moved closer to him and pointed her finger at his chest. "You're welcome? I can't believe you. You've just made me lose my daughter to that bastard and you want me to thank you?" she reprimanded.

Andrew stepped closer, closing the gap between them. "No, I saved her from that bastard. You were going to sign over your rights to him without so much as a fight."

"How do you know I haven't put up a fight? You don't know me. You don't know what I've been through. How can you just butt into something you have no clue about?"

"Nyla, I know exactly what's going on. You were about to sign a document that would have robbed you of your rights to ever see your daughter again. Do you know that? Did they tell you that? Did you even bother reading what you were about to sign?"

Nyla didn't answer, but the look on her face told him everything he needed and already knew.

"Yeah, see what I mean? They knew that if they scared you enough, you would sign anything without question."

Nyla shook her head as tears started to pool in her eyes. "No, that's not true. Robert wouldn't do that to-"

Andrew couldn't help but frown. "Please, Nyla, you're smarter than that. You know damn well he would. Hell, he was about to."

"But he said…"

Andrew bent his knees in order to meet her eye-to-eye.

"He said what? That you guys could work something out later, just sign this now and in, let's say a month or two, you guys could start talking about visitation?"

Andrew watched as tears began to fall from her eyes as she closed them. A shudder wracked her body as he knew the truth of his words finally hit home.

The bitterness of her reality choked Nyla as she tried to swallow her shame. How stupid could she have been? Robert didn't have it in him to do right by her. Deep down in her soul, she knew that, but she couldn't help herself. She wanted to believe that she was wrong. Nyla had a big heart. She tried to see the better in people, believing in giving second chances to right wrongs. It was the idea of giving people just enough rope to hang themselves that drove her. However, she gave Robert too much rope, and instead of hanging himself, he used the extra rope she gave him against her.

Andrew, feeling the anguish that started to engulf her, moved his hand to the side of her cheek and wiped underneath her eyes. He shifted his other hand to the left side of her cheek and repeated the gentle touch.

Seeing her broken, exhausted and deflated, he heard himself say to her, voice low but strong, "I'm sorry this is happening, but I'm not sorry for butting in."

She opened her eyes, looked up at him, and he could see, *truly see*, just how much she'd been raked over the coals by Downs. He hated what he saw in her eyes. She was giving up, but he wouldn't let her.

"I will not let them take her from you, I promise you that," he assured her. "I will do everything in my power to make sure that doesn't happen. Whatever it takes..." He paused, and keeping the connection with her, added, "I know I'm asking for a lot, but I need you to trust me. Can you do that?"

They watched each other; Andrew trying desperately to convey that he'd meant her no harm, that she could trust him, and Nyla was doing everything in her power not to melt in his arms. She knew the moment that he sat down next to her and took over the meeting that she could trust him. She felt it the instant they first laid eyes on each other. But she needed to be a smart woman. Her past failures couldn't be repeated by trusting someone blindly. That didn't work for her in the past, so what assurances did she have that it wouldn't happen again?

That's simple, she told herself, *This man is nothing like Robert.*

It was the way he looked at her, how he was touching her that made him different.

Finally, Nyla nodded and replied softly, "I trust you."

Relieved, Andrew swallowed the urge to seal this moment with a kiss. He stepped back from her, reached into his inside suit jacket and produced his wallet. He pulled out his card, which read his personal information and phone numbers, and handed it over to her.

"You get off at three, right?" he asked. Nyla nodded and he continued, hoping she didn't realize he knew her schedule. "Okay, my office address is on this card, along with all of my phone numbers. Come by my office right after work so we can get started."

Nyla shook her head. "I have to get my daughter right after work. I don't-"

"That's fine. Bring her with you. I don't mind. Just be there today after work." He moved past her and realized that half of the wait staff and the cook were all staring at him. He ignored them, turned, and instructed, "Make sure you do not speak to anyone but me or my assistant, understand? No one is to call you. If they do, give them my name and number and instruct them to call your attorney."

Nyla frowned and shook her head. "I don't even know your name. I mean, I..." She looked down at the card, reading his name, then back up at him, and for the first time since she'd known him, he smiled.

"It's Pierce. Um... Andrew. Andrew Pierce. I'll see you this afternoon, Nyla Montgomery."

* * *

THE MOMENT JOHN MICHAELS and Robert Downs made it to their cars, Robert looked at his lawyer over the hood of his Bentley.

"So, that's it? We're just going to tuck our tails in and run?" Robert bit venomously.

John had paused before he opened his own car door.

"Yes, we are. You don't want to fuck with Pierce. Hey, I'm ruthless and, if I had more time, I could probably come up with something to handle this but Pierce; man, he'll come up with something more that will bury you alive. I'm not trying to get into a fight with him; not over this. You lost Robert; take that shit like a man. I'll call you when I schedule a meeting."

Robert watched his lawyer climb inside of his cheap ass Lexus and drive away. Robert turned his attention back on the diner.

I be damned if I'm letting this shit ride, Robert thought.

Robert Downs didn't know the meaning of losing. As he started the motor of his car, he thought of a plan that would teach that smug lawyer and that stupid cunt bitch just who *he* was.

CHAPTER 3

Nyla crawled out of her old, beat up Dodge and ambled toward the door of Mama Joe's Daycare Center.

The rush of the door as she opened it brought the screams, laughter and cries of about forty little ones to her ears.

She smiled. She had missed her little girl since the moment she dropped her off this morning. Se'Nya was her life. She'd never imagined that anyone could make a baby as wonderful as her ten-month-old, much less herself, but she had. She was a beautiful, chunky baby with golden brown skin, wild, curly, light brown hair and big questioning gray eyes that had the power, it seemed, to look straight through you.

People had told her that some babies had the knack to sense evil in others. Just how dogs could smell fear on people, babies could sense when a person didn't have a pure and good heart. Nyla felt her baby had that gift. She didn't care for strangers at all and didn't trust anyone until she was around them for a long time. If she didn't get a good vibe from a person, she'd let you know.

Nyla shook her head and chuckled softly at a painful revelation. If only Se'Nya could have warned her about Robert, she'd probably be better off. Nyla stopped at the infant room and peered through the glass door. Se'Nya was sitting in one of the bouncers, smashing her juicy hands on the buttons surrounding her. Nyla smiled as she watched her.

"She's beautiful just like her mother," said a deep voice behind her.

Nyla jumped slightly, not from the unfamiliarity of the voice behind her, but his closeness. Nyla turned and looked up into a set of deep brown, almost black eyes. They were smiling at her as she relaxed.

"Hey, Darrius. What are you doing here?" Nyla asked.

Darrius Clint gazed into her hazel eyes as the swell of his chest prevented him from taking a breath. He pushed her hair from her eyes, a cancellation prize for what he truly wanted to do. There was no doubt in his mind that he wanted her. Unfortunately, he had yet to see his affections returned.

"I'm here to pick up Baby Girl. Remember you asked me this morning if I could pick her up for you?"

Nyla stared at Darrius for a moment before she closed her eyes and groaned. "Oh, yes, I do remember. I'm so sorry. Today was the day from hell, so Rock let me off early, and I completely forgot to call you."

Darrius frowned. "Yeah? What happened at work today?"

Darrius and Nyla met four years ago when she first moved into her current third-floor apartment. Darrius no longer lived in her building, but he made it his mission to see her every chance he got.

For years, Darrius had been a good friend to her. He was always there when she needed someone and never minded it, especially when Nyla became pregnant with Se'Nya. He was there for the late night cravings, Lamaze classes, and Nyla's bouts of depression when she realized she would be doing this alone. Darrius was also the first one to see Se'Nya when she was born.

Nyla loved Darrius. He was one of the few people in her life that she could count on, that she could depend on. It was Darrius and Dee Dee who continued to be there for her. She trusted them with her life, something that she didn't do lightly.

A few of her friends, as well as Darrius', had questioned their friendship. They wondered why Nyla and Darrius hadn't taken their relationship to the next level. For a while, they both would say that they were just friends and that their friendship was too precious and good to taint. But, recently, she could see that Darrius no longer felt that way. He was becoming clingier and more demanding.

Nyla knew that Darrius was a catch. Darrius was very attractive with a hard muscled body to boot. He was past six feet, with dark skin and beautiful white teeth. His smile was charming and could render a woman helpless with said charm. If you meant something to him, he would do anything for you. If he didn't like you, you knew it. His parent's taught him how to treat a woman right. He was respectable. He'd open doors, give you his coat if you were cold, and made sure you were well taken care of. He was a woman's wet dream, especially when he wore basketball shorts. From the look of the calm swell in the front of his shorts, there was no mystery that the man was gifted.

Nyla's friends, especially Dee Dee, also thought it was insane that Nyla hadn't jumped on Darrius. They called her a fool for passing a chance to potentially be worshipped and pleasured every night of her life.

Unfortunately, Nyla just didn't see Darrius like most women did. She wanted more than just the physical desires that an attractive man evokes. Nyla felt like Darrius wanted to be with her, and granted she *did* love him, but she wasn't *in love*. Nyla believed in love at first sight. She thought she had that with Robert, but eventually learned that what she was feeling was the excitement of a man like him wanting her.

After a few months into the relationship with Robert, she knew nothing would come of their relationship. She wished she had broken it off with him sooner. But, if she had, she wouldn't have her baby girl. She wasn't sorry about having her daughter, not at all.

Darrius shifted his weight, trying to hold back his growing frustration with this woman before him. If she would just get a clue and cooperate, shit would go so easy for her. He looked through the glass window at Baby Girl and grinned. For that little girl's sake, he'd have to make Nyla see that he knew what was best for them, before it was too late.

Darrius put his arm around a cagey Nyla and broadened his smile. "Hey, why don't I take my two favorite ladies out to eat? You can tell me all about your day, and I can get my time in with both of the women in my life."

Darrius didn't wait for her to respond. He quickly opened the classroom door and went straight for Se'Nya.

Nyla watched for a second as Se'Nya stared at Darrius as if she didn't know the man. He talked to her a bit and made her laugh before he picked her up.

Huh? That was strange.

Se'Nya had been around Darrius all of her life, and yet Nyla had never noticed her behave that way towards him before today.

"Maybe I'm just tired," Nyla wondered to herself.

When Nyla walked into the room and her daughter saw her, Se'Nya squirmed frantically, trying desperately to get to her mom. She cooed, laughed, and reached out for Nyla.

Nyla laughed and took her daughter in her arms.

Darrius smiled. "She must have missed her mama."

Nyla kissed her daughter on her cheek and held her close, breathing in her daughter as the feeling of home took hold of her.

She asked Darrius, without looking at him, "Does she always treat you like that when you come and get her?"

Darrius shrugged. "Most times, but you know how shady she can be." Darrius hustled to the door. "Come on. Let's get something to eat. I'm starving."

Nyla watched him go, then looked down at her babbling baby. Nyla kissed her forehead. "You're not shady. Are you, sweetie?"

In answer, Se'Nya gave her a wide toothed grin and smacked her face.

* * *

THE MOMENT NYLA ARRIVED HOME, she dropped heavily onto her couch. She had been going for over twelve hours and needed to get off of her feet. She had to practically beg Darrius to take them home instead of getting ice cream. She had had a long and stressful day. All she wanted to do was relax before she had to do it all again tomorrow.

Darrius had taken them to a buffet restaurant, one of Darrius' favorite places to eat. The moment they sat down and she told him all about what happened; she wished she kept her mouth shut.

She had to listen to Darrius go on and on about Robert, how he wasn't shit, how her taste in men sucked. She didn't tell him about the help from Andrew or what that help meant to her; she just mentioned she ended up finding a lawyer to help her. When Darrius asked how much the lawyer was going to cost, she really didn't have an answer. She just told him that that would be worked out tomorrow. In truth, she had no idea. It wasn't something that she and Andrew had talked about, and when she spoke to his assistant today, Bertha, it wasn't mentioned then either. She had every intention of talking to Andrew about everything, but when she arrived to his office Bertha told her that he got called away for a meeting at the court house. For a split second, Nyla let the seed of doubt plant in her mind that he really didn't want to help her. However, she quickly dismissed that idea. She truly believed that if Andrew didn't want to help her, he wouldn't have stepped in at all.

After Nyla bathed and put Se'Nya to bed, Nyla googled Andrew Pierce, Attorney at Law. Thirty-minutes later, she was more confused than ever. There's no way he would be able to help her. He practiced corporate law, not family law. She also knew, from just reading about who he worked for that she would not be able to afford him.

She started to panic. What if believing in a man she knew nothing about was the biggest mistake of her life, again? A lump caught in her throat as she thought about losing her one true reason for living?

She shook off the fear of the possibility.

I need to think this through.

As she showered and climbed into bed, she tried to convince

herself that declining Andrew's help was the best thing to do. However, as she settled deep into her pillow, she knew it wouldn't be that simple. Andrew had been the focus of her deepest desires ever since she laid eyes on him. His strength, his demeanor, and his adverse confidence that threatened to choke everyone around him was sexy as hell to her.

The way he took charge and put both Robert and his high-priced lawyer in their place; man, if she wasn't so freaked out and scared, she would've jumped him right then and there. She was attracted to him; there was no doubt about that. But it seemed to be more than that. She felt a stronger pull toward him today, something that she had never felt before. She would always get nervous when she was close to him, but for some reason, today it was stronger, and it seemed to get stronger the longer he stayed close to her.

She'd been thinking about the tender way he touched her all night it seemed. She hadn't thought about anything else but how good it felt to have his hands caressing her, creating an abiding need to have him in between her thighs. She felt wrong for having these feelings for someone that she *knew* belonged to someone else. It wasn't her style, but for some reason, she couldn't help herself. Of course, she would never act on those feelings, but oh how she wanted to. Just looking into his eyes, she wanted to believe that he wanted her just as much as she wanted him. She wanted to believe that the gentle way he looked at her meant he felt the same as she did.

All of it was wishful thinking though. The cold and harsh reality of it all was that he was taken. He had someone that wanted him as desperately as she did. Nyla saw it written all over the woman's face; besides the appalling expression that she held the moment she entered the diner.

What Nyla should be doing, she discerned, was to try to open herself up to Darrius. He wanted her; she knew this without a doubt. He would be able to take care of her and Se'Nya with no problem. Darrius wasn't a lawyer, but he had a great job driving for one of the top shipping companies in the U.S. He could provide for them and she liked him. But she didn't want to simply like someone, she wanted to be in love. She wanted her soulmate. And the only man she felt that passionate, deep emotional connection for was for the one man she couldn't have.

"Andrew…"

CHAPTER 4

*A*ndrew ran his hand through his hair as he headed to his office. He was exhausted. So far he'd been busy in court all morning, and once he made it back into the office, he found himself in meetings with his other clients for the remainder of the day. He loosened his tie a little and took another deep breath. Finally, he had the chance to relax. That's when Nyla Montgomery entered his mind.

He couldn't believe how much he wanted and needed to see her again. He wanted to satisfy the sudden urges to be with her, but most of all, he wanted to feed his curiosity. He had so many questions to ask, most of them centered around her and Robert. It didn't take long for him to learn all he needed to know about what happened between the two of them. His office was a gossip train filled with more rumors than the tabloids. It seemed everyone knew about this mess except him. Andrew learned that Nyla had suffered her reputation because of her relationship with Robert. After all, Robert was a married man.

There was no way he could be certain that Nyla knew Robert was married. He just had a feeling that she was innocent in all of this. Andrew had known Robert Downs for years, and during that time, he had never seen the man's left ring finger decorated with the symbolic band. The flip side of that was Robert's evil bitch of a wife, Debra. She had no problem showing off her seven carat diamond every chance she got. However, the miserable couple never made appearances in public together, unless it was for an A-class crowd.

Which bodes the question of how Nyla and Robert met. These two were from different worlds. They didn't socialize in the same circles; they didn't have the same friends. From the stories he'd heard, they met at a function both attended and Robert was the aggressor.

Robert was known to sleep around on his wife, so Andrew believed what he'd heard. He also believed that fucking around on his wife was a game to Robert. He'd even witnessed Robert on the prowl before, stalking after women. He couldn't keep his dick in his pants, but Andrew figured Debra didn't care as long as she wasn't embarrassed. So when it got out that Nyla was pregnant by her husband, that he'd fucked up by embarrassing his wife and family, Andrew heard that Debra didn't take it well, and hell, neither did Robert. Being the bitch that Debra was, she defamed Nyla so bad in the press that she became the home wrecking whore that had come between a "committed marriage." *Yeah right!*

Robert, of course, had played the innocent victim. He let his wife run Nyla, the mother of his child, into the ground without a second thought. Nyla being the mother of his child should've meant something, but it meant shit to Robert. Andrew felt his jaw tense as he thought about how Robert let this happen. It pissed him off to no end to hear how Nyla was treated, and even though he didn't know much about Nyla or the situation, he believed in his soul that she deserved better.

He frowned and berated himself. He should have beat the shit out of Robert in the diner when he had the chance. But knowing Robert the way that he did, Andrew knew that he would have his chance again. It was inevitable.

"Hey, Pierce." Andrew stopped walking after hearing his name and looked into the office of Lazarus Spencer. Spencer was a co-worker who Andrew fucking despised but tolerated. Spencer was a decent lawyer who was part of the family law division within his firm.

Spencer was just as tall as Andrew but three times his size with small, unwelcoming eyes. He couldn't understand why Spencer even practiced family law. He had admitted multiple times, to anyone who listened, how he hated children.

Andrew walked into the man's parse office and gave a head nod. "What can I help you with?"

Spencer smiled and leaned back in his screaming chair. "Heard you have quite a case on your hands."

"Where did you hear that?" Andrew frowned, thinking about the Buckman case that was just wrapping up. "The Buckman case is actually cut and dry. The lawsuit has no merit. It should be wrapped up in a few days."

Still smiling, Spencer shook his head. "No, not the Buckman vs. McManus International case. I'm talking about the Downs case."

Andrew's brows furrowed, instantly on high alert. "What about the Downs case? What have you heard?"

Spencer stood and walked around his massive desk. He leaned against the desk and folded his arms in front of his meaty chest.

"Oh, I haven't heard any particulars. Just that you've got yourself wrapped up in some shit, that's all." Spencer started to laugh. "Wow, this is crazy. I've never heard of so much fuss over a little ass. I mean sure, she is hot as hell, but I didn't think she was all that. I wonder what she did to get you involved in this. It must have been big." Spencer then leaned closer to him and grinned. "Tell me, did she drop to her knees and wrap those fantastic thick lips around your-"

Andrew didn't let the man finish. Before Spencer was able to blink, Andrew was on him. He'd quickly grabbed Spencer by his tie and pulled his body toward him. "Go ahead and finish. What you were going to say?"

Andrew, keeping a tight hold on the tie gripped in his hand, forced Spencer back against the nearest wall. The rage was welcomed as he slammed the overweight man against the wall and lifted him a few feet from the ground.

"Jesus Christ," Spencer's scratchy voice spat, thrashing his legs.

"Tell me what you know," Andrew growled.

"I don't know anything," Spencer strangled out before Andrew tightened his grip further.

Andrew stared in the man's eyes as his predatory features came alive. He knew that if he didn't keep it together, things could get much worse very quickly.

Andrew spoke in a carefully controlled tone. "You must think I'm a fucking fool, Spencer. You know something, you son of a bitch. Spill it."

Spencer, trying desperately to remove Andrew's hand from his favorite tie and breathe at the same time, saw something in Andrew that he never saw before. He knew the man was crazy, but he figured it was rhetorical in a sense. He didn't believe it was actually true. He did now.

"You're crazy," he managed to force out.

Andrew, however, didn't care too much for him breathing any longer. He kneed him in the nuts and tightened his hold on the tie, completely cutting off the man's air. Spencer's face started to turn dark red.

"You will tell me what I want to know or so help me God, your fucking days of living will be over."

Andrew didn't have time to play games. It would be a matter of seconds before all hell would break loose and he broke this man's neck. Andrew was about to cross the point of no return, and Spencer felt it too. He nodded quickly, signally he was ready to talk and Andrew finally released him, letting his feet finally touch the ground.

Andrew stepped back to give Spencer room but not enough to get free of him.

Spencer bent over coughing. "I can have you arrested and disbarred," he said in between breaths.

Andrew frowned. "Please, you fat fucking prick, I know a lot more judges than you. Trust me, you don't want to go there."

"You tried to choke me, you bastard!"

Andrew actually grinned. "No, I don't recall that. Besides, you know how you're into that kinky style BDSM fucking. You probably have your Dom tie you up around your neck or something and beat the shit out of you on the regular."

Spencer frowned, instantly bringing his hand around his burning neck. He released his tie and opened the top button on his shirt.

"Please, I'm not into that shit."

Andrew shrugged his shoulders. "Oh, but you will be if you keep fucking with me. I'll have witnesses, pictures and video that say otherwise circulated faster than it would to take your fat fingers to lift a donut to your mouth."

Spencer stood upright quickly and met Andrew's crazed eyes. The truth in them, the calculated madness that was displayed all over Andrew confirmed what Spencer had thought earlier. The man was certifiably crazy. One thing Spencer wasn't was suicidal.

"Now, tell me what I want to know… now," Andrew charged.

When Spencer didn't respond right away, Andrew growled and moved to grab him again. Spencer held his hands up and backed away. "Okay, okay! I'll tell you, shit. What do you want to know?"

"You know exactly what I want to know. You're stalling, and I'm losing my patience."

Spencer went to his chair and sat down. He shakily took a bottled water from his desk, unscrewed the cap and took a healthy gulp. He pulled out another one and handed it to Andrew. Andrew shook his head, knowing those bottles had anything but water in them. He could smell the alcohol from where he stood. He sat down in front of the still red-faced Spencer and waited with narrowed eyes. Spencer was an opportunist, not a gossip. He'd always been like that. He only gets involved in shit that benefited him. If it didn't, he didn't give a damn what went on around him. The revelation that Spencer was a greedy bastard and seeing the fear that was dripping off of him told Andrew that Spencer was more involved in what was happening between Nyla and Robert than he was letting on.

Outwardly shaking now, Spencer took another drink from the water bottle. He could feel the beads of sweat forming above his brow, pooling under his arms.

Shit, this fucking lunatic, Spencer spat to himself.

"Pierce," he said finally. "I don't know much, but I can tell you what I've heard."

"Why don't you tell me how you're involved with Downs?" Andrew charged.

Spencer's eyes grew as he shook his head vehemently. "I don't know what you're talking about. I-"

In a blink of an eye, Andrew had sprung to his feet and lunged for Spencer over his desk. Spencer reacted but not as fast as he would've liked to as Andrew grabbed a hold of his tie again. Spencer shot up, as fast as his bulk allowed, and stepped back from his desk, letting Andrew pull his tie off his neck, tripping over his chair and almost falling to the floor.

"All right, all right! Damn it, Pierce!"

Andrew clenched his hands into tight fists, imagining exactly how he would throw this fat fuck out of his office window. Would he bust the glass first or just use the momentum of Spencer's body to do the work for him? He smiled wickedly as he decided exactly how he would do it.

"What the fuck did you do, Spencer?" he asked as he sat back down in his chair, dropping the tie on the floor next to him.

Spencer placed his hands up in an effort to calm the rage that was evident in Andrew's eyes.

"All right, look; I overheard Robert talking one day at some fundraiser event downtown. He mentioned that he got this waitress pregnant and she was keeping the baby. He said that he told her he wasn't leaving his wife for no simple ass. He bragged to a few people, telling them that he said to her 'if you want to have the baby, you're on your own' and that he wasn't getting involved. Someone asked him what would happen if she tried to take him to court, and that spooked him."

Spencer then leaned forward and placed his meaty hands on his desk. "Pierce, if only you could have seen the fear in his eyes. You know how much of an asshole Robert is, right? I even heard you two got into it a few times. So, yeah, I started thinking what if I could expose him for the scum of the earth that he is?"

"So you decided to reach out to this innocent woman and you what? Told her you would help her get support from her baby's daddy?"

Spencer shook his head. "Okay, no, that's not exactly how it went down. Look, I figured this would be a way to get back at him, you know? So, I leaked the information about him having a kid by another woman to the right people in his circle. Then I went to find her to try and talk her into taking him to court. I figured if I made him look like shit in the public eye, then maybe that precious reputation of his would fall apart."

Andrew grunted, seeing exactly how things played out. "Only the shit has backfired," Andrew added, and Spencer nodded.

"Yeah, in more ways than one. First, she wouldn't cooperate. No matter what I said to her, she wouldn't take my advice. Something about Robert had too much power or some shit. I tried to tell her that together we would take that power from him but she didn't listen. She just wanted to stay under the radar and away from Robert. What she didn't know was that her little secret wasn't a secret any more. The cat was out of the bag."

"Did you tell her that?" Andrew asked.

"I didn't see a need at the time. I figured once word got around, he would do whatever it took to bury it. He would quietly pay up to keep her quiet and of course, I'd get a piece of the pie from the woman since I was advising her, but that didn't happen."

Andrew frowned. "It sure didn't. Instead, Debra made this innocent woman out to be a home wrecker and Robert an innocent victim and now he's trying to take her baby from her."

"Yeah, that was the other thing that blew up. But come on, do you really think the girl was innocent in all this?"

Andrew's demeanor quickly changed and Spencer started backpedaling fast. "Okay, yes, she probably was innocent, but I was trying to look out for her. I had no idea Downs would react the way he has. Shit," Spencer chuckled uncomfortably, "He has a fucking hard-on for this case. He turned the tables and started making her out to be a horrible person for keeping him from his child. It's a mess." Spencer ran his hands through his thinning hair.

"So what's your plan to clean this shit up?" Andrew asked.

Spencer shrugged. "What do you expect me to do? I mean, I tried to help her and when I knew I couldn't, I told her to find someone else that could. I sent her in the right direction; that's all I was able to do for the girl. I wouldn't go near this with a ten-foot poll, and anyone that represents her from here on would be committing career suicide. Do you know Michaels is Downs' attorney? That's why I'm trying to warn you, Pierce. I know you are good, but going up against Michaels *and* the Downs'? I mean, can your reputation withstand this? It's really fucked up. Look, man, take my advice and let this go. I heard Michaels gave her a chance to save face and make this situation better for all parties. Just advise her to take the deal and be done with this."

"Oh, so, I should just let her give up the rights to her child to Downs? I don't fucking think so." Andrew stood. "I want everything you have on this case sent to Bertha within the hour. It shouldn't be much since you haven't done shit but fuck a good person."

Spencer rolled his eyes and mumbled, "Yeah, I wish."

Andrew's features frowned and Spencer wisely pushed himself against the window behind him. He inquired quickly, "So, you're taking her case? You're doing it pro bono?"

Andrew ignored him and added, "Don't let me have to come back here if I don't have all the information I need in my hand in the next fifty-six minutes."

Spencer's meaty neck shook as he nodded. "Oh, you'll have everything you need."

Andrew moved to the office door, then turned and said, "Oh, and Spencer, if I find out you were involved in this shit deeper than what you told me, I will break your fucking neck, understand?"

Spencer replied, nodding his head quickly, "Perfectly."

CHAPTER 5

Forty minutes later, Bertha, his assistant, bounded into his office with a slim folder in her hand and slammed it on his desk.

"What's the meaning of this? I hear you're doing work for free? What's in it for you?"

Bertha Swan had been Andrew's assistant for years. She'd been with him and seen him through a lot of difficult issues in his life. She and Andrew's relationship was different. They were more like brother and sister than employee and employer. Bertha was the utmost professional at doing her job, however. She had Andrew running like a well-oiled machine. However, when they were alone, she had no problems lighting into him like she was doing now.

When Andrew first met Bertha, he was astonished at how her name didn't match her physical appearance at all, but it fit her loud voice and big personality. Bertha was a very attractive woman with light brown skin and long hair that she always kept in a tight ponytail or bun. She was tall; about as tall as Andrew with her heels on. She had a figure that any woman would kill to have.

Andrew took the folder that she'd slammed on the desk and

opened it. The first thing he saw was a picture of Nyla and a beautiful light-brown skinned little girl with light brown, curly hair.

Bertha folded her arms over her breasts. "When do you think you'll have time to do pro bono work?"

"I'll make it work," he told her as he kept his eyes on the photo.

He could see the resemblance between mother and child, but he didn't see Robert anywhere in the little girl's features. As his eyes studied the picture, he still felt that passionate magnetic pull toward Nyla. He also felt the happiness radiating from her eyes just by looking at this picture.

Unfucking believable.

"Earth to Andrew."

Andrew pulled his attention from the woman in the picture and looked at the angry one before him.

"Can you please explain to me when you started back working on child custody cases?"

"Since right now," he replied, finally removing the picture in order to start reading the file.

"So it's true?" she asked him.

Andrew looked up puzzled. "What's true?"

"That you have lost your god damn mind!"

"No, Bertha, I haven't." he breathed exasperatedly. "This is just something I have to do. It's a sensitive case, and she needs me."

"Oh, *she* needs you?" Bertha challenged.

Andrew realized the implication of what he said and looked up into Bertha's questioning brown eyes.

Andrew leaned back in his chair and took a deep breath. Another job Bertha had was keeping him in line when he was teetering on the crazy and insane. Their relationship gave her the means to call him on his shit without reproach. She knew all of his secrets, even the dark ones. He tried to run her off like he did the others when he lost his wife, but Bertha hadn't budged. She stayed by his side no matter what happened, and he loved her for it.

Andrew didn't reply to her. His eyes simply conveyed what his mouth didn't. The softening of Bertha's face told him that she got it.

She sat down in one of the chairs facing his desk. "Tell me," she said simply.

So he did. He told her everything, from the moment he saw Nyla a month ago, how he continued to go to the diner every morning just to see her, and how he'd been unable to think of anything else but her. He described the connection he felt with her and how he'd barely summoned the control to keep himself from claiming her.

Bertha watched her boss talk about this woman with a fire in his eyes she hadn't seen in a very long time. She was just as shocked by his behavior as he was. Bertha knew a lot about his marriage to the one woman Andrew believed was his lifeline. When he lost her suddenly, he lost himself too. He claimed he would never be the same again but as she sat before him, that clearly wasn't true.

Bertha asked, "Do you believe she had no idea Robert was married?"

Without hesitation, Andrew nodded. "I do. You don't know her, Bertha. I can see Robert taking advantage of her completely, making her think she was special and only using her for shit only knows what."

Bertha rolled her eyes. "Oh, I know what, and if you'd like, I can tell you so you'll know too."

Andrew put his hands up. "Ah, no thank you. It was a figure of speech."

Bertha smiled and shook her head. "You know this is going to be a fight, right?"

Andrew nodded, bringing his steeple fingers to his chin, "Yes, I know it is. It's nothing I can't handle."

"Yes, but will she be able to?" Bertha said pointedly, and he paused a bit. He knew he could protect her and knew he would do anything it took to do it.

"I'll protect her. She won't be a casualty here and neither will her daughter. I can handle this."

Bertha scoffed. "You can handle this? *Please.* You couldn't handle lame ass Spencer telling you the shit that he heard about her without you choking him out. If this ever went to court-"

"This wouldn't make it to court."

"Yeah, but think about it. What would happen on the off chance it did? There would be bodies left in your wake all because someone implicated something about her that you didn't like."

Bertha could see the rage fueling within him, threatening to come out that very moment. His eyes suddenly took on a different form and quickly changed colors before they went back to their natural state.

Bertha wasn't afraid of Andrew; she was more afraid of what he may do if he ever lost control.

"Andrew, I know you know what you're doing. My concern is the fact that you have deeper feelings for this woman, more than you clearly had with Mikaliah, I really think you need to take a pause here."

Andrew frowned. "What do you mean by that?"

She sighed. "Just hear me out, okay? You almost lost it three times because of this woman. Two times you almost killed three people in cold blood, and even though they all probably would have deserved it, no one would understand. She has a hold on you. You haven't let the darkness consume you in a very long time. If you even saw someone bump into her by accident, you'd probably lose your damn mind. That's emotionally involved, Andrew. You're too close to this. You need to step back and give this to someone that you trust."

Andrew tried his best to remain calm. Bertha was only telling him what he knew deep down to be true.

"And who do think I should illicit help from?" he asked.

Bertha smiled and folded her arms over her chest. "Baby, the fact that you've asked that question tells me you are not playing with a full deck." She stood. "Look, you are the best at this very thing. Playing dirty is your specialty, so I know you can make sure Downs doesn't hurt your girl or put his greedy little hands on that precious baby. I also know you will make Michaels eat shit and die. But you could do even more damage by getting the help of a certain woman that you know to make sure Michaels and Downs get exactly what they deserve."

Andrew couldn't help the shit-eating grin that suddenly appeared as he understood exactly what Bertha was implying.

"Yeah, I think you have a point. Get her on the line will you?"

Bertha smiled. "With pleasure."

CHAPTER 6

"Lori, I'm not in the fucking mood," Andrew barked as he removed Lori's hand from unzipping his pants.

They were sitting on the couch in his office. He was nursing a scotch, and Lori was trying her best to get Andrew aroused.

Lori would typically wait until after work hours, and after his cock-blocking assistant left for the day, to see him. Andrew worked late the majority of the time. Other than meeting him at the diner in the mornings, this was the only other time she got to see him. If she wanted to get to him, get some from him, she had to go to him.

She knew A.P. never minded her unexpected, late night visits to his office. It didn't matter what he was doing, the minute she walked into his office, he was on her, ripping at her clothes, trying to get to her. She loved his hunger and insatiable nature. He was a fantastic lover. She did want more from him besides sex, but she would also take whatever she could get. He was just *that* good.

However, tonight he wasn't biting. She'd arrived at his office wearing a trench coat, heels and nothing else, and yet he hadn't touched her.

Lori frowned and leaned away from him. She knew something was going on with him. No matter the man's mood, he was always put together. His blonde hair was always neatly in place. He kept his suit jacket on while he worked in his office most of the time. If he did take off his jacket, or his tie, his shirt would remain neatly tucked into his pants. However, when she walked into his office, Andrew's jacket was strewn across one of his chairs facing his desk. His tie was gone, and his shirt was hanging loosely around his hips, completely unbuttoned. His hair was tousled from the continuous raking of his hands through his locks, which made him walking sex and had her dripping with need.

Yes, something just wasn't right. A.P was the epitome of control, but right at this very moment, she noticed, for the first time, that control was nonexistent. He was tense and distracted. He needed to relax and get refocused. This was her chance. She would prove to him that she could be the woman he'd been looking for. She would do whatever it took to make him see. Whatever it took, she was willing to do it to make him hers.

She slowly caressed him with her eyes, admiring the sheer perfection that was his body. Lori raked her nails down the ridges of his t-shirt, feeling the deep valleys between his chest muscles and the eight-pack abs that she marveled at every time they made love.

She also felt a deep rumble underneath her hand right before a vice-style grip encircled her wrist.

"What did I just say?" Andrew quipped.

She snatched her wrist away. "A.P., what's going on with you? Why are you like this? Why don't you let me help you? We haven't fucked in days." Lori purred and smiled, opening her coat to him, "Let me give you what you need."

Andrew looked over at her but didn't reply. *Damn, it's been that long?*

"I told you," he replied tersely. "I'm not in the mood."

And he wasn't. No, he'd been going out of his mind thinking about someone else entirely.

Now that he'd taken on Nyla's case, he'd been working nonstop. He hadn't been to the diner in a few days and he'd missed her the afternoon that he told her to come to his office. He was pulled away for an emergency meeting for one of his cases and had to let Bertha take care of her. He was pissed as hell but tried to convince himself that it was no big deal that he hadn't seen her, but he knew it was a lie.

He was going out of his mind. He hadn't been able to concentrate fully for days. He'd been extra aggressive, cold and heartless to everyone around him, coworkers and clients alike. And, even though his clients and bosses loved how he was behaving, he didn't.

For the past few hours, he'd tried to focus on work. He needed to prepare for court in the morning, and he was having a hell of a time completing his tasks. He needed a distraction, and as if on cue, he saw his office door open and Lori glided in wearing nothing but her coat and red heels.

Lori was hot as hell, and she was right; any other time, his cock would've been massaging her pussy right this very moment. But he lied when he told her he wasn't in the mood. He was, he just wasn't in the mood for her. He *wanted* to be in between a woman's thighs, feeding his sexual urges and tension. Sex had always been his way of relaxing, and since he was always tense, he had sex a lot. Andrew didn't ease into any woman's pussy, though. He was selective, and most times, Lori was who he went to when he wanted meaningless sex. But since that day at the diner, since he touched *her*, all he wanted was *Nyla's* sweetness glistening all over his dick and no one else's.

Frustrated, Lori stood, wrapping her coat around her naked body. "This is bullshit. I could be doing better things with my time than wasting it on you."

Andrew rested his head against the couch and closed his eyes. "Then go do it."

Pissed, Lori crossed her arms in front of her. "Are you serious?"

"Oh, as a heart attack."

"If I leave, I'm not coming back."

"Have a good night," he countered before he brought his glass to his lips.

"As a matter of fact, I've been asked to go to the Caribbean for the week," she told him, trying her best to get the response from him she desired.

"Oh yeah? Have a safe trip," he mumbled.

Lori stared at him as confusion, frustration and disbelief filled her. Her frown deepened as she spat, "You are such a fucking asshole!"

He scoffed. "Yeah, so I've been told."

"Argh!" she screamed, taking off one of her shoes and throwing it at him.

Andrew jumped up, dodging the collision, and had to quickly stop himself from ripping her apart.

"What the hell is wrong with you?" he snapped.

She pointed her manicured finger at him. "Is this how you're going to treat me? Like I'm nothing to you? After everything we've been through, after what I put up with, this is how you're going to treat me. Like I don't matter?"

She moved closer, nose flaring, eyes but slits underneath her brows. "Do you have any idea what you're turning down? Do you think you're the only show in town? That men aren't knocking at my door?"

"Do you think I give a shit?" Andrew raged, apathetic of subtlety. "Lori, you and I aren't together. We will never be together. I've told you this countless times, and every time you've assured me that you understood."

"Yeah, well, what did you expect? I thought you would change your mind."

He shook his head. "Oh, please, you know damn well there was no way in hell I was changing my mind. First, we are not compatible. Do you think I want an evil, unemotional woman for a wife? Do you think I want to start a family with someone like that?"

She snorted. "Are you kidding me? As evil and heartless as you are, do you expect *me* to believe that *you* want a family? You want kids?" She laughed bitterly. "Get real. You aren't capable of that shit. Umph.... I don't see how your wife put up with your shit, but lucky for her, she doesn't have to anymore since she'd dead."

Lori folded her arms, satisfied that she was able to dish as much venom as she could, but she quickly started backing up from him as she realized she'd gone too far.

Andrew could feel his entire body convulse with suppressed rage. The tension in his jaw tightened as he saw nothing but red. He knew that he was on the brink of fucking losing it!

"Get the fuck out," he demanded.

"Andrew..." she started, realizing what she had done.

"Out!" he boomed, sending him spiraling out of control. If she didn't leave now, she wouldn't be able to on her own.

Lori jumped clear out of her skin from the sound that permeated from this charged animal. She knew she'd gone too far, but she didn't expect him to react this way. She thought about trying to apologize again, but the look that suddenly appeared on his face made her skin grow cold.

It was too late; she needed to leave now. Lori hobbled quickly to grab her purse and shoe and made it out of the door just in time to hear a large crash behind her.

CHAPTER 7

*A*ndrew had to calm down; otherwise, he was going to lose control and rip his entire office to shreds. Lori was being a bitch, he knew, and he also knew it was because of him being an asshole. But, the way she spoke about his wife hit a nerve. Sometimes just talking about his wife or thinking of her took him over the edge.

He closed his eyes trying to relax, trying to get himself together, but he kept hearing her words repeated over and over in his mind. *"You want a family? You want kids? Get real with yourself. You aren't capable of that shit."*

Hell, maybe he wasn't, and that thought alone was keeping him in his rage-filled state. There were times where he thought he lost his wife because he didn't deserve her. He didn't deserve the promise of the life he was going to have with her. The reality that she was taken away from him ate at him every day.

Andrew moved to his desk and placed his hands on the cold wood. He closed his eyes and tried to concentrate on something, anything, to calm him. He couldn't think of shit. Then suddenly it happened. Just before he was about to give into his rage, his mind shifted to *her*. He took a deep breath as a now familiar feeling took over. Fuck, he wanted to see her. He could sense her presence, which he thought was impossible, but his body reacted as if she was right outside his door. His breathing picked up with anticipation. Her familiar scent consumed him, tempted him.

What was she doing to him?

His chest swelled as the uncontrolled need to dominate came over him. Andrew quickly grabbed his desk phone. He had to see her. Maybe that's what his body was telling him; he needed her.

Just as he began to dial, he heard a knock on his office door just before it opened.

"You just don't listen, do you?" he seethed, turning toward the door waiting to see Lori's face appear.

It wasn't her.

Nyla jumped slightly from the sound of his voice and explained quickly, "I'm sorry. The door was partly open. Um, if you're busy I-I can come back."

Andrew didn't reply. Instead, he took her in as his heartbeat settled, as the pulse in his neck subsided, and as his breathing finally came under some type of control. He wasn't completely in control. It's just something that he'd grown accustomed to feeling when it came to her. What he had noticed, however, was how the predator in him silenced.

Nyla asked hesitantly, as she slowly moved toward him. "Are you okay?"

Andrew rested his behind on his desk and continued tightly gripping the edges of the wooden furniture.

"What are you doing here?" he asked, voice edged with tension, not bothering with answering her initial concern.

She paused and watched him for a moment. "I ....uh ....was in the neighborhood and thought I'd stop by," she sighed. "You haven't been to the diner in a few mornings, and I... well, I wanted to check up on you." She pointed to the door behind her and added. "I saw your girlfriend leave. She seemed upset. Did you two have a fight?"

Andrew started to call her reasoning for coming bullshit. He could sense she was holding back but something else she said registered louder and he frowned. "My what?"

"Your girlfriend. You know the blonde that's always with you at the diner? I don't know her name…"

"Lori," he offered as he watched her nervously watching him. She looked as if she was holding her breath waiting for his reply, which she was.

Nyla smiled, rubbing her clammy hands against her jeans. "Yes, that's her. I mean, I'm assuming she's your girlfriend." She giggled as her eyes darted everywhere around the room, avoiding his heated, steady gaze. "Why wouldn't she be, right? I mean, you seem like a man that has good taste. And she's pretty, right? A little too rigid and cold in my opinion, but maybe you like that kind of thing…"

She was babbling. It didn't matter how much her brain was telling her mouth to shut up, her lips just kept moving. They couldn't stop.

Andrew's eyebrows rose in amusement as he fought the grin that was beginning to take form. Nyla went on and on, anxiety covering her, as she talked about his taste in women, how Lori seemed like a lovely girl in all so she saw how he would want to be with her.

It was all bullshit, but he didn't want to tell her just yet. He enjoyed hearing her fumble around, trying to hide what he undoubtedly knew. She wanted him just as much as he wanted her. He knew that he made her nervous; he noticed it every time she stood next to him to take his order at the diner. He enjoyed watching the nerves fall off her in waves. She was a complete and utter turn on.

He openly raked his eyes over the tan jacket that stopped at her waist, the white form fitted V-neck style t-shirt and dark skinny jeans, all which hugged her generous breasts, hips, and thighs nicely. She dressed up her feet with black high-heeled shoes, adding the sex appeal that was Nyla. Her eyes and lips were dressed too; nothing too overt, but were subtle and warm, with light color above her eyes and shimmery light gloss on her lips.

Now *this* was the distraction that he needed.

He cleared his throat and brought his eyes back to her bright ones. "Lori isn't my girlfriend," he admitted finally.

Nyla paused in mid-babble and stared at him. "W-what? She isn't?" her voice queried softly.

"No, she isn't."

"Oh, I thought because she was always with you…"

Andrew ran his hand through his hair and rested it against the back of his neck. "Yes, well, I can see why you would think that, but no, she isn't my girlfriend. In fact, I don't have a girlfriend."

"You don't?"

He shook his head. "No, I don't."

"Oh," she answered softly as her mind started going double time to match the rhythm of her heart.

Nyla couldn't believe what she was hearing. Was it possible that her dreams were actually coming true?

"What about you?" he asked.

"Me?" she blundered, bringing her right hand first to her throat to massage the muscles there, then to her chest, covering her out of control heart.

Andrew grinned slyly and lifted himself from the desk. "Yes, you. Are you single or do you have someone special in your life?"

Watching him stalk toward her naturally made her step back slightly from his pursuit. "No, I-I don't have anyone special."

He stopped in front of her and tilted his head to the side. "Why is that?"

She blew out a sigh and shrugged. "I don't know. I guess I haven't found the right person, or I'm a repellent for good guys. Who knows?" She looked at him questioningly. "Why do you ask? I mean, why do you want to know if I have anyone special in my life?"

"I was just wondering, that's all. Just making sure…"

Andrew abated his eyes from hers again so that he could drink her in from head to toe, letting his desires for this woman show all over him.

"Oh? Y-you were wondering about what may I ask?" she asked him softly.

"Who I had to get rid of so I can have you to myself."

Nyla's breath hitched softly, but Andrew caught it. When he met her eyes again, they were wide as saucers. He smiled at her. "Did you think I went to that diner just for the omelets?"

Nyla bit her bottom lip and shook her head. "Well, I....um..."

He tilted his head to the side again. "Please, Nyla, I can make an omelet ten times better than that cook of yours. That wasn't the reason why I went there every morning, or why I sat in your area so you would be the one to wait on me."

Nyla was at a loss. She couldn't move her lips to formulate any words and her brain was trying desperately to control her heart from bursting out of her chest, to keep her lungs working, and her legs from giving out.

Andrew, seeing his goal unfold before him, moved closer to her. This time, she didn't move. She looked up into his eyes and watched helplessly as he invaded her personal space.

"Why did you come here?" he asked her again, closing his eyes and inhaling her scent.

Just what I thought, he said to himself. *She does smell like fucking chocolate.*

Nyla closed her eyes as a shaky breath released from her parted lips. Goodness, his closeness was doing a number on her. She clinched her thighs together as she tried to gather herself.

Before she could think, she said softly, "I needed to see you."

His eyes shot open and his eyebrows rose in surprise. So did hers, for that matter, and she back peddled quickly. "Y-You know," she stuttered, "T-To talk to you. I needed to see you to talk to you."

What is he doing to me?

So close; God, he was so close that she could feel his heart beating against his chest. His breath tickled her neck, encouraging her desires, her urges, her commands to let go. The need to give herself to him was taking over.

Andrew, not able to hold back any longer, bent slowly until his lips were inches from her neck. He inhaled again. *Yes!*

"Nyla," he whispered against her neck right before he lightly brushed his lips against her smooth skin.

Fuck, he was straining to keep himself under control.

Just for a little while longer, he coached himself.

"Yes?" she replied, closing her eyes and trying her best not to lose it.

"Why are you really here?" he probed breathlessly against her neck before he leaned back slightly to look at her.

"Um... I..." She risked looking in his eyes and knew instantly, by the hungry heated look saturated in them that she was in deep trouble. She bit her bottom lip, preventing the hitching of her breath from being unleashed.

Andrew couldn't resist her any longer. He brought his right hand up slowly, and the moment he touched her chin, he exhaled coarsely, as if he'd been holding his breath this whole time, anticipating touching her.

"What is it about you that has me losing control; that has me thinking of nothing else but you?"

She shook her head slowly, her voice lost in her closed throat.

Andrew continued to slide his fingers along her jawline, around her neck, until they found their way just under the base of her skull.

"Do you know what I haven't been unable to stop thinking about?" he asked her, hearing the ache in his voice no matter how much he tried to remain in control.

Nyla, oblivious to what was happening to him, shook her head. "No," she said finally. "Tell me."

He let out an exacerbated and lust-filled sigh just as he snaked his arm around her waist, bringing her body flush up against his.

Nyla gasped lightly, her lips parting slightly, as she finally felt *exactly* what she was doing to him.

"How good you would taste," he confessed in a discreet whisper right before he descended closer to her. The grip on the back of her head tightened and shifted until his fingers were in her short hair.

Nyla closed her eyes, anticipating the touch of his lips, hoping it would be everything she imagined it would.

Oh, please let it be, she prayed.

The moment Andrew's lips latched onto hers, every inch of control they both were desperately trying to hold on to was now gone.

Nyla sighed, opening to him the second he gripped her hair so tight that it was on the verge of pain. She gripped his biceps, frantically trying to keep herself upright. The strength in her legs gave way with every stroke of his tongue against hers.

She moaned deeply into his mouth and felt his grip on her tighten.

Andrew pulled back suddenly and wildly looked into her lustful eyes.

"Fuck, Nyla, you taste as amazing as I knew you would," he breathed, voice husky and low.

The power this woman had over him still astounded him. He always remained in control, keeping his shit together at all times no matter what. But this woman, this beautiful being was taking control of him. His need to have her, his yearning for her was clouding all rational thought.

Kissing her, tasting her, didn't do anything but make his appetite for her drive him out of his damned mind.

"More," he declared as he slowly removed her jacket from her arms.

As the jacket fell to the floor, Nyla moved her arms around his neck and threaded her fingers through his silky hair, creating a tight grip of her own. The four-inch heels she wore didn't bring her where she needed to be so she moved to the tips of her toes and brought his lips to her. She kissed him deep, trying urgently to brand her body to his. She felt his hands roam her body, rubbing her back, arms, face, and gripping her ass.

Andrew, needing to feel her, yanked her shirt from out of her jeans. His heated touch against her body caused her to moan again; damn, she couldn't help it. She'd longed for him to touch her, for him to kiss her for so long that her senses were in overdrive.

She should've stopped him. Hell, she should've slowed him down, but as his hands shifted up her back to unclasp her bra, there was no way in hell she was stopping him now.

Andrew took one of his hands out from under her shirt and gripped her ass tight. He lifted her so she could wrap her legs around his waist.

"Drew," she whispered against his lips.

This is happening. Oh my. This is indeed happening, she thought.

Andrew growled and walked her to the nearest wall. Once her back was up against the cold wallpapered surface, he greedily pulled her shirt and bra up, revealing the beautiful balls-throbbing-sight that almost made him explode in his briefs. He moved her body further up his chest and didn't waste time as he insatiably took one of her supple perked nipples into his greedy mouth.

"Have mercy," she told herself as she closed her eyes and let this man take from her body whatever he wanted.

She grinded against him, feeling the need between her thighs grow. Her lips pulsed greedily, hoping *his* lips wouldn't forget their hidden existence, longing for the feel of him skin to skin.

"Andrew, please...," she panted softly, while keeping a tight hold of his hair.

Andrew sucked, pulled and played with each nipple. Hearing Nyla moan, thrash and call his name over and over again only fueled him to do more, to claim more.

He *needed* more.

Andrew brought her bruised lips to his and kissed her again, slower this time. Shit was about to get interesting, and he wanted her to know first and foremost how out of control he was, but at the same time show how desperately he wanted and needed her. This wasn't something that he wanted to end after tonight. She was his, and he had no doubt in his mind that he would be hers.

Feeling that things had escalated to another level, Nyla undid her legs from around his waist and slid down his torso. She surveyed her mind, waiting for that voice to tell her to escape now while she could, but she heard nothing. In fact, her heart pulled her closer to him. She wanted more of him. So help her, if she didn't have him, she didn't know what she would do.

Andrew, seeing the desperation in her eyes moved back from her body slightly, giving himself just enough room to unbutton her jeans.

"Are you soaked for me?" he asked, panting slightly as he unzipped and spread the top of her jeans apart.

He groaned just as he pushed his hand down the front of her pants until his fingers touched her slick warm folds. Nyla gripped his arms tight at the sudden invasion.

"Shit, baby," he breathed as he teased her swollen lips with just a finger, lightly grazing her swollen clit up and down, feeling her body shudder with every sweep. He circled slowly, determined to tease, to build, to drive her insane.

She started to moan, a sound that drove him to tease her more. The sound of his name floated sensually from her lips and caused his dick to scream for release. Damn, he needed more. He pushed one finger, then two inside of her channel and was rewarded enormously by the clamping of her walls against his fingers. Her grip on him was so tight that her pussy seemed to not want to let him go.

Andrew slid his other hand around to the back of her head, gripping her tight as he took her pussy with just his fingers. He salaciously moved in and out of her, determined to make her lose her mind, burning with the need to taste her desires on his tongue.

"Oh, yes," she cried passionately, keeping her eyes on his, watching him lose control with just his fingers inside of her. "Yes, Drew. Oh, please, baby… Oh, yes. Please…" She bit her bottom lip and moaned slowly, letting her head lull back. She was building. She felt it in the pits of her stomach.

She started circling her hips against him, tightening her walls even further.

"Fuck, Nyla," he panted and pulled his fingers hastily from her precious sweetness.

He gripped the sides of her pants and pulled them down from her waist just as he walked her backwards. He lowered her as easy as he could onto his couch and quickly brought her panties and jeans to her ankles.

From that point, he was gone. No longer was he showing control. No longer was he showing restraint. No longer could he wait. Fuck removing her clothes the rest of the way. Fuck removing her shoes. He pushed her legs up and back, touching her knees to the couch, a spot just above her shoulders. She was sprawled out for him and he couldn't take his eyes off of her. She looked so fucking sexy, just as he imagined she would. The moistened lips that he'd been teasing, that he'd been drumming, were smiling back up at him, calling for him to lap every single drop of her juices.

Nyla tried to push herself up, releasing her from the way he had her pinned to the back of the couch, but he wasn't having it.

"I have to taste you, baby; I have to. If I don't, I'm going to fucking lose it," he declared miserably as if he felt a pain so strong that it would destroy him.

Before Nyla could respond, Andrew moved his head between her thighs, resting the back of her knees on his shoulders and buried his face in between her folds. Nyla gasped loudly as his tongue swept against her clit, instantly threading her fingers tightly in his hair.

"Yes, baby, I love when you do that. Hold on to me, baby," he announced right before he ravaged her pussy like a sustenance deprived beast hungry to survive.

She had never in her life been ravaged this way before. She'd been with a couple of men in her life, and they all had gone down on her, but it was never like this. They never savored her, they never claimed her the way that Andrew was right now.

She tried to bite her screams, but it was impossible. Andrew didn't let her. He went in on her with abandonment, with a voracity that even he had never felt. And when she came, when he drank her desires, he knew there would never be another woman that would bring him to his knees like this one.

"Off, Andrew," Nyla growled, grabbing his shirt, then his t-shirt, and pulling them away from his body. "Now, Andrew, Take it off now... Please, baby. Oh, please, Drew..." she began to beg.

He didn't listen. He could feel her building again. He could sense that she was just on the verge of...

"Ohhh my fucking... Baby... Ahhhh!" she screamed as her orgasm gripped her whole body while she exploded. She sat up after she gathered herself, trying to push him away from her and declared with a pained voice of her own, "If you don't take your fucking clothes off this minute, I will rip them off myself."

Andrew couldn't help but release the hold he had on her clit and laugh.

Nyla brought both of her hands to his face and pulled him closer. She kept her eyes locked on his dark, hooded blue ones and for the first time saw some specks of red in his irises.

"How long are you going to make me wait?" she asked him. "I need to feel you inside me, baby."

"Well, that will depend on how long you can get your ass dressed and in my car."

Her eyes bulged. "What?"

Andrew touched her lips with a lone finger before he told her, "Baby, I will not take you for the first time on my fucking office couch. I've been waiting for this moment for too damn long. I plan to have you naked, sprawled and panting for my cock in my bed. I want to take my time and cherish this beautiful hungry pussy of yours."

Nyla shook her head. "Damn, you're sexy."

He grinned and leaned into her just to get another taste of *his woman*. He then reluctantly moved from between her thighs, his heaven, and pushed her panties back up before he helped her with her jeans.

"Do you have a restroom close by?" she asked, shyness quickly taking hold of her.

"Yeah," he stood, not caring if she saw the tent in his slacks, and pulled her up. He guided her to a door on the other side of his office, opened it and turned on the light.

She smiled and was about to thank him when she heard her phone ringing in her jacket. Andrew moved to retrieve her jacket that was still lying on the floor and brought it to her. Nyla pulled out her phone and saw that it was Dee Dee. Nyla had asked Dee Dee if she could watch Se'Nya for a few, while she came to speak with Andrew about her case. She told her it wouldn't be long but after what just happened, she thought of asking if she could stay *just* a little longer.

"Hey, girl," she answered. "Is Se'Nya okay?"

"Not sure, honey. She's fussier than when you typically leave her with me. She felt a little warm, so I took her temp, and it was hitting close to the hundred mark. I gave her some baby Tylenol, but you know ain't nothing like mama's arms."

Nyla looked into Andrew's eyes as she spoke on her phone. "Okay, girl. I'm on my way." She hung up and looked apologetically at Andrew.

Andrew feeling her apprehension asked, "Is everything all right with Se'Nya?"

"I'm not sure. She has a temp of about hundred."

Andrew's eyebrows rose. "Seriously? Do you need to take her to the ER?"

Nyla shook her head as she reached behind her and clasped her bra back. "I don't think so. She's had fevers before from a cold or an ear infection. I'll call the doctor on my way home and see if he wants to see her."

"What can I do?" he asked her.

She smiled and touched his face. Just hearing him offer his help warmed her. "Nothing, but thank you for offering."

"Nyla...," he began as he placed both of his hands on her face. "Anything you need, don't hesitate to let me know, understand?"

"Andrew, that's sweet of you. You are doing too much as it is."

"I disagree. Let me lock up my office and walk you down to your car."

She waited as he grabbed his jacket, some papers from his desk, briefcase and turned off his office light. He reached for her hand and guided her through his office to the bank of elevators. He kept her close to him as they rode down.

"Where are you parked?" he asked her.

She told him that she parked outside of the building on the street and he directed her out of the elevator, passed the overnight security and out the front door.

"Call me when you get home," he told her, kissed her chastely, and stepped back as she got inside of her car.

As Nyla watched Andrew disappear in her rearview mirror, she couldn't help the huge grin that transformed her face. What had both happened and almost happened was unbelievable and completely surprising. Her reason to see him had everything to do with her case and nothing with her sexual fantasies about doing lustful and ravenous things to him or even what he could potentially do to her.

She was elated that he was single. She was excited that he ended up having the same type of feelings for her as she had for him. What made her smile and happiness fade was her case. Would he be able to be with her *and* represent her too?

"Shit."

She couldn't worry about it now. She needed to get to her baby, then figure out how to talk to Andrew about him representing her. She didn't want it to look like she was giving him sexual favors for his help. Maybe a payment plan or something could work. She laughed out loud and shook her head.

Yeah right. I can only imagine what he would take for payment of his services.

And, oh, what services it was.

He was a silver-tongued devil on all fronts. He was definitely skillful and remarkable. She wanted to know what else he was remarkable at doing, but as she thought about it further, she wondered if they could mix business with pleasure. Would it be a conflict of interest? Would she be able to hold back her need for him to touch her again to kiss her, taste her?

"Hell no!"

CHAPTER 8

The moment Andrew made it home from seeing Nyla at his office, he tore off his clothes, took a cold shower, and tried to take his mind off of what had just happened.

However, as he collapsed on his bed, naked, his mind went back to the feeling of her lips. He reminded himself of how soft they felt, how expertly her tongue moved with his. It was rhythmic, sultry and fucking hot as hell. When he finally got his hands and lips on her body, on her breasts, it was just as he knew it would be. She felt incredible against his touch. Her skin was soft and warm. Her curves drove him insane, and he couldn't slow down from feeling and tasting more of her.

Just thinking about her, her body, her scent, had his dick hard as a rock. The soft way that she moaned into his mouth, how she grinded her body in time with his tongue, drove him crazy and was doing a number on him now. He started stroking himself slowly, closing his eyes and picturing Nyla, how fucking good she tasted, how wet she was for him, how she clamped tight against his fingers, his tongue. He remembered how soft her skin was when he touched her, how her smile would light up…

Yes, there it is, he said to himself as his hand moved faster and faster. He licked his lips still tasting her on his upper lip as the scent of her desires still resonated on him, in his nose, in his mouth, in his soul. She was what he wanted. She was what he needed. She was…

"Fuck!" he yelled, as me moved faster and faster until finally… temporary sensual bliss.

Andrew laid there a moment, cum dripping down his stomach, threatening to drip on his sheets. His breath was coming fast, heart beating out of control, but he had the largest smile plastered on his face. He got up, careful not to lose his boys on his sheets and cleaned himself off.

If he didn't get to her soon, he and his right hand were about to be best buddies and that hadn't happened since middle school. When he lay back down on his bed, he reached for his phone. He noticed he missed her call while he was in the shower, but she texted him that she made it home safely. As he stared at her message he knew he wouldn't be able to sleep until he heard her voice. Hoping she'd still be up, he looked up her number and pressed the call button.

"Hello," a soft voice answered.

He closed his eyes and practically melted in his pillow at the pure sound of her voice. "Hey, it's A.P. or …Um…It's Andrew."

She chuckled softly and his dick twitched.

Fuck!

"Yes, I know who this is. Your name is programmed in my phone; besides, I know your voice."

"I hope you don't have my number under asshole," he said both jokingly and seriously.

Nyla chuckled again. "No, I have you under Drew."

"Screw you?"

"No, silly. *Drew*," she laughed.

He grinned and closed his eyes feeling as giddy as a high school boy finally talking to the girl he'd been crushing on since forever. He draped his arm over his eyes and asked, "Do you have a moment to talk?"

"Yes, I'm just lying in the bed. I've been having a little difficulty falling asleep."

His eyebrow rose, hearing the hidden message in the inflection of her voice. "Really? Thinking of me?"

A soft, "Yes," came breathy and low from her, and Andrew almost told her that he was on his way to her.

Instead, he said simply, "Good, I haven't stopped thinking about you since the first day we've met."

Silence greeted him, but he expected it. For him, the shit that was happening between them was getting deeper by the seconds, and he didn't care. It was about time.

Breaking the silence, he asked, "How's Se'Nya?"

She sighed, "She's better. Her temp is down, and I finally got her to sleep. Hopefully it breaks tomorrow and I don't have to take her to the doctors."

She proceeded to tell him all about Se'Nya as he got comfortable in his bed. He listened intently, asking questions when he needed to, but other than that he just listed to this woman express to him how much she loved her daughter. It made him smile, but it also made his heart ache for what could have been.

"Drew?" she called to him after he failed to answer her question.

"Yes? Sorry, sweetheart. What did you say?"

"I asked you to tell me more about you. Considering you know more about me than most- Hell, more than a lot - I just wanted to know more about Andrew Pierce."

He chuckled. "What do you want to know?"

"I don't know. Everything. Tell me about your parents. Do you have any siblings? What made you become a lawyer? You know, stuff like that."

"Okay, well, my parents are still living. They live on the outskirts of town. I have one sister who's older, way older, so we don't have that much of a connection and six brothers."

"Dang, six brothers?" Nyla asked.

"Well, they aren't biological, but they are as close to me as brothers could be."

"Oh, okay. Are they like your foster brothers or something?"

"Something like that, yes. What about you?"

"Me? Well, it's sort of like you, except I'm on the opposite side of things. I was the foster sister of some. I don't really know what happened to my parents. The earliest I remember is being raised by my grandmother, but she died suddenly, and I was placed in the system. My foster families didn't have any back stories about me, and I tried to find out all I could about my family but didn't have any luck."

Andrew sat up a little and placed his pillows behind his back and head. "Hey, I can probably help you with that."

"Really? How?" she asked him.

"A few of my brothers are in law enforcement. They would have the means of locating anyone. If you have your grandmother's name and where she used to live, they could probably get you the info you need."

"Seriously? And you don't mind asking them for me?"

He could practically feel her excitement and hope through the phone. Hearing her happiness made his chest swell. He knew there wasn't anything that he wouldn't do for this woman, and he almost told her this.

Again, he kept those feelings to himself and replied, "No, I don't mind, and they wouldn't mind doing it either. Just let me know."

Smiling, she answered, "Thank you. I will."

There was a slight pause before Nyla confessed. "Andrew, I don't know if I said this to you already, but I really appreciate you helping me with Robert. This situation between him and me is really screwed up, and I hate that Se'Nya is caught in the middle of everything."

"Hey, I'm just glad I was in the right place at the right time, that's all. Don't worry about anything Nyla."

"I'll try not to," she told him. She then asked hesitantly, "Do you... um... know what happened between him and me? Well, I'm sure you have considering who Robert is."

"No, actually I hadn't heard anything before I took your case. But yeah, I know a little now, and I guessed the rest."

She groaned, almost as sexy as she had earlier. "I must sound like an idiot to you or something else entirely."

"Neither actually. You didn't deserve to be treated the way you did by Robert and his bitch of a wife. Remember, I know Robert. I know how much of an idiot *he* is; I know how much of a *pussy* he is."

"But you had to have heard the rumors that I was 'sleeping around with a married man knowingly and that I trapped him.'"

He sighed, biting back the sudden surge of anger that was rising within him. "Yes, I've heard that, but I don't believe it. I think Robert sold you a dream, and you had no choice but to accept it. I think he used you for whatever he wanted, and when he realized how special you were, how he didn't deserve to breathe the same air as you, he let you go. I know his punk ass never told you that he was married. If he had, you wouldn't have given him a second thought, and that would have fucked with his self-esteem."

Nyla lay on her back and looked up at her ceiling. "Yeah, well, tell that to his wife. She's called me everything but a child of God in the press and to anyone who'll listen. I hadn't been in this city for that long, only about four years now, but I had heard of the Downs. However, I didn't know Robert was the son of the great Richard Downs. The day I met him, I had no idea who he was. He told me his name was Robert Manns. I knew he was a business man, but that was about it." She sighed through the phone, remembering how stupid she felt when she realized Robert's real name was Robert Mansfield Downs. "I tell you, that man put me through a lot. I want to say I wish I never met him, but that would mean I wouldn't have Se'Nya, and she's such a gift."

Andrew internally sighed. He didn't want to admit it, but he was glad to hear all of this from her. It just solidified what his heart was telling him.

"Yes, she is," he told her. "And she deserves the best. Again, don't worry about him. I'll take care of everything. Now, enough about him. Tell me what you're wearing."

Nyla laughed aloud and quickly covered her mouth, hoping she didn't wake Se'Nya.

"You are such a perv," she replied, her cheeks burning from smiling so much.

"Oh, baby, you have no idea."

Andrew kept Nyla on the phone for as long as he could, asking her about her life, her likes, and dislikes. He wanted to get to know everything he could about this woman. He told her about himself but never brought up Mikaliah.

Not yet, he told himself. *But soon.*

When he finally hung up, he needed to take another cold shower before he was finally able to sleep.

* * *

THE NEXT DAY, Nyla sat in a booth at work anxiously looking out of the window for Darrius. He was bringing Se'Nya to the diner so that Nyla could take her to the doctors in a few hours. Nyla was first going to call off work today in order to take Se'Nya to the doctors, but Darrius offered to watch her until she got off work.

"There's no reason for you to miss out on your pay and sit around waiting for an appointment," he told her. "I'll watch Baby Girl until it's time and bring her to you."

Nyla told herself that if she saw any hesitation in his daughter when Darrius came to her house, she would tell him never mind. But Se'Nya was fine. She went to him with no problem. Nyla was truly grateful for Darrius, but she didn't think relying on him would be appropriate any longer, especially since things seemed to be happening with Andrew. She would have to talk to Darrius sooner rather than later.

Dee Dee walked into the diner for her shift and smiled when she saw Nyla. She didn't get a chance to talk to Nyla when she came home to take care of her daughter last night. This was the perfect time to get the scoop about her meeting before her shift started. As always, as she surveyed the diner, it was packed.

Dee Dee groaned, *This is going to be a long night.*

Nyla smiled as Dee Dee approached.

"Hey, girlie. How's Se'Nya?" Dee Dee asked, sliding into the booth across from Nyla.

"She still has a fever. I'm waiting for Darrius to bring her here. We have an appointment in a few hours."

Dee Dee smiled. "Speaking of gorgeous men, we didn't get a chance to talk last night. How did everything go with your meeting with Mister Wonderful?" She then leaned down and grinned devilishly. "Did you exchange sexual favors for his help?"

Nyla's eyes practically jumped from her sockets, and she looked around the diner checking conspiratorially.

"What do you mean by that? Dee Dee, I would never…"

Dee Dee laughed and touched Nyla's shoulder. "Girl, I was kidding. I know you wouldn't do anything like that. I was just messing with you."

Relief suddenly flooded Nyla, but her reaction wasn't lost on Dee Dee. She knew Nyla. The careful way she was looking around the diner, as if someone was watching them, told her that Nyla was hiding something and it was good.

Dee Dee studied Nyla as she asked. "Hey, did something happen between you and Mister Wonderful? Did he renege on helping you?"

"Did who renege on helping you?"

Both Nyla and Dee Dee looked up and found Darrius looking down on them with Se'Nya squirming in his arms.

Nyla, ignoring Darrius, stood and reached for her baby.

"Hey, love bug," she cooed and kissed her daughter. "How are you feeling, honey?"

Darrius looked at both women and realized that they were going to ignore his question. However, as he looked at Dee Dee, he knew he'd learn soon enough. Darrius slid into the booth, sitting across from Dee Dee. Nyla slid into the booth next to Darrius.

"Thank you for bringing her here and I really appreciate you watching her for me."

Darrius smiled at mother and daughter. "You know it wasn't a problem, baby. Anything for you Ny."

Darrius turned his attention to the other woman at the table and smiled.

"Sup, Dee." He nodded.

Dee Dee smiled, pushing her black hair behind her ear. "What's up, Darrius?"

Dee Dee scooted out of the booth and stood. She bent over and pulled Se'Nya from her mother's hands. "Hey, baby girl. How's my girl, huh?" Se'Nya looked at Dee Dee intently and started babbling. Dee Dee smiled. "I know, honey. I promise to take better care of you next time you get sick on my watch."

Darrius instantly frowned. "What do mean by that, Dee? Were you with Se'Nya last night?"

He didn't let Dee Dee answer before he looked over at Nyla. "Nyla, if you needed me to watch Baby Girl, I would have. You didn't need to have Dee Dee drive way across town to do it."

Nyla sighed and looked at Darrius. "I know, and I really appreciate all the help you give me. Dee offered, okay? She's also letting me use her car while I run some errands today before I head home."

His frowned deepened. "Yeah, and I could have taken you anywhere you wanted to go too. Damn, Nyla, you know I got your back."

Darrius put his arm around her shoulder and threaded his other hand through hers. Nyla looked deep into Darrius' eyes and held her breath.

Please don't say what I think you're going to say.

He never got that chance. Her baby girl let out a loud screech of excitement that startled her as well as Dee Dee. Nyla looked up at her daughter and found she was fighting to get away from Dee Dee. Se'Nya was leaning forward, arms outstretched toward someone that Nyla had never expected to see today. Her heart started picking up speed from just the sheer sight of him, the promise of his presence, his touch. She remembered how it felt when he touched her. When he kissed her, sending her in a lustful haze spiraling out of control.

And, oh my, that tongue of his. She shivered at the memory as her core immediately started heating up.

Never in her wildest dreams did she think he would have reacted to her that way. He took over her body as if she belonged to him from the moment she was born.

And late last night he had called her, something that she didn't expect. She called him when she got home, but he didn't answer his phone. She left a message never expecting to hear from him but she was very happy she did. He talked about nothing and everything, learning what he could about her. He asked about her daughter, asked about her past. He wondered if she was okay, if he needed to come by and take her and Se'Nya to the ER so Nyla wouldn't have to worry about driving.

He listened for at least an hour as she told him all about Se'Nya's past illnesses without a fuss. Nyla was falling for him worse than she imagined. Before they hung up, she told him that they needed to talk. He agreed, but couldn't give her a timeframe on when he would be free. She told him to let her know so she was completely surprised to see him walking through the door. She was also surprised that he wasn't alone.

CHAPTER 9

Andrew couldn't stop what was happening even if he wanted to. The jealousy, the enthralled rage within him was boiling out of control. Just the sight of the man sitting next to her was causing him to lose it. The fact that someone was touching what was his was sending him into orbit. He could feel the shift within. The darkness getting stronger.

"Andrew, what the fuck!"

He didn't feel her hand on his arm until she started applying pressure, until he felt her nails dig into his arm.

Andrew turned his attention from Nyla to Elese's panicked gape.

"What?" he growled uncontrollably.

Elese, his best friend's sister, shook her head and moved to stand in front of him. "Get control for shit's sake. What's wrong with you?"

Andrew's frown deepened. "You don't see what I see? Nobody touches what's mine, Elese."

Elese looked into Andrew's eyes and saw something that she hadn't seen in a very long time. She had known Andrew all her life. He had been her brother's best friend since they were kids. In all the years that she'd known Andrew, he'd never sparked this out of control. They would always tease him, saying that he had OCD or something; he was that controlling. Nothing caused him to lose it, no matter how angry he got, he stayed in control. However, what she was witnessing right now scared the shit out of her.

She looked over at the booth, at the woman that was the reason for the lapse in his judgment, and gasped lightly. Andrew had told her a little bit about the feelings he had for her, which was why she was here, but she never expected to feel something too. Elese felt as if she had no other job here but to protect this woman from, shit who Andrew? No, what she sensed from him wasn't threatening to Nyla. She took another sweep of the diner but couldn't discern where the threat was coming from but she hadn't mistaken the feeling, no the *need* to protect her.

The anger, the fury Andrew was giving off was getting stronger. It was clear that things were far worse than what he told her.

She could see the wrath deep in his eyes. What in the hell was she supposed to do? She hadn't had very much experience dealing with Andrew and his temper. Her brother was the one, the only one that could calm Andrew.

Elese tried to say calmly. "Let me go over there and settle things."

"There's no need. I can handle it," Andrew told her and started around her, but she moved to the left, blocking his departure.

"Bullshit, you can handle it. At the state you're in, you can't handle breathing. Just take a moment, Andrew, please?"

Andrew looked down at Elese. "The longer I stand here, the worse off everything will be. So if you don't want that, I suggest you get there before I fucking do." Andrew bit out forcefully right before he headed for Nyla.

"Shit," she mumbled under her breath as she trailed after him.

Where the hell is my brother when I need him?

Nyla watched the interaction between the blonde woman and Andrew in amazement and shock. Andrew was standing tall in a dark gray suit, white crisp shirt, and gray and blue tie. The woman was dressed in a light gray suit and a soft pink blouse. Her slacks were slim in cut, which contoured her shapely legs. The jacket came in expertly, accentuating her slim waist. It wasn't lost on her that this woman was a knockout.

What also wasn't lost on her was her inability to calm the beast that was Andrew Pierce. She could see from where he stood how dark his blue eyes were, how his brows were wrinkled in vexation and his jaw was clenched so tight that he was turning red, literally.

His rage wasn't intended for her, she noticed. No, it was aimed directly at the man sitting next to her. It was that moment that she realized the temperature in the room seemed to elevate ten thousand degrees.

Andrew Pierce was jealous!

She could feel Darrius tense as he met Andrew's gaze with a little heat of his own. She quickly realized if she didn't do something soon, World War III would break out in seconds.

"I'll be right back," she announced quickly, pulled herself away from Darrius while keeping her eyes solely on Andrew. "Keep Se'Nya with you, Dee Dee," she added as she passed her.

Nyla wasn't sure if she would be able to stop Andrew, but just in case she didn't, she wanted to make sure her baby wasn't caught in the middle of a testosterone induced massacre.

Andrew saw her coming toward him with trepidation in her eyes. He knew she didn't understand what he was capable of, but from the look in her eyes, she had an idea. She was coming to calm him, but as she got closer, it only made things worse. It was a different kind of uncontrollable fury that his senses were succumbing to. It was dominance, it was lustful aggression, it was his burning desire for what he couldn't fucking live without.

Just as Nyla got close and brought her hands up to ease his temper, Andrew snaked his arm around her waist, lifted her slightly and brought his hungry lips to hers.

He familiarized himself again with her taste, with her mouth and took what he'd been craving for since last night.

Nyla felt her body hover over the diner floor, but she thought it was just the result of Andrew taking her mouth in the most dominant way a man could ever claim a woman. Her panties had to have melted off her hips; there was no other way that they could've stayed covering her soaked core.

Nyla laced her fingers through the man's hair moving her tongue rhythmically with his until he finally pulled back. When he released her lips, he didn't move far from her. They both could feel their quickened breath teasing each other's faces as they both fought to gain control.

Nyla took a few seconds to catch her breath, to will her heartbeat to slow down and her body from going into shock. "Fuck, that was amazing," she said softly.

She felt his body shake before she opened her eyes. The smile that greeted her that very moment, a smile that reached his expressive, deep blue eyes, made her insides turn to jelly.

Elese couldn't move a muscle in her body. She was mesmerized by what she'd just witnessed. She'd seen Andrew with other women before. Hell, his late wife was her best friend. She'd seen them together all the time. Observed the love he had for her, how he treated her, protected her, adored her. But as she watched Andrew look heavily into this woman's eyes; how he held her tight against him as if he never wanted to let go, she knew she just witnessed something profound, something beautiful. She also knew she needed to call her brother. He needed to know what happened here. He needed to know about this woman, about Andrew's woman, because she believed it finally happened.

He'd finally found her!

Elese smiled as she watched Nyla look into Andrew's eyes with the same amount of intensity, passion, and possessiveness as Andrew had in his.

"I see someone has some jealousy issues," Nyla breathed out.

Andrew grunted, still holding Nyla tight against him.

"No one touches what belongs to me, Nyla," he told her as he slowly placed her feet on the diner floor.

"And I take it I belong to you?" she tested, biting her lip.

Andrew rested his hand at the base of her skull and gripped her head tight. "Baby, my face has been buried in your pussy. I've sucked, licked, and fondled parts of you that I know very few have seen or have been. I'm addicted to your taste, beautiful. You damn right you're fucking mine!"

"Agh! Really, Pierce," Nyla heard a voice say next to them but she ignored it.

She was too busy fighting the urge to claim Andrew's sinful mouth again. Nyla ran her hand through his hair and rested it at the back of his neck while the other hand rested on his chest.

Her face then opened up to one of the warmest smiles Andrew had ever seen.

"Aww, that is the sexiest thing anyone has ever said to me," she teased, but she meant every word.

"Oh yeah," he began, "wait until I sink…" Andrew abruptly heard a sound of someone clearing their throat next to them as Elese threw up her hands saying, "Give us a break will you!"

Nyla and Andrew finally turned their attention away from each other and found Elese and Dee Dee standing next to them. Elese greeted them with a huge smile on her face while Dee Dee stood next to her with a fidgeting Se'Nya.

"Someone was getting a little antsy over there." She replied sheepishly.

Nyla smiled, let go of Andrew and went to grab her daughter, but Dee Dee pulled her back from Nyla.

"Nope, suga, it seems she has her eyes set on someone else."

Nyla dropped her arms as she indeed witnessed her pride and joy practically fall out of Dee Dee's arms and grabbed Andrew's suit jacket.

Andrew's eyes moved to the little girl with the most beautiful gray eyes he'd ever seen. Andrew stood stock still and looked at Nyla.

Nyla smiled. "You better take her. She's a stubborn little girl, and if she doesn't get her way, she raises holy hell."

Andrew reached for Se'Nya and pulled her into him. It had been a long time since he'd held a baby, but he quickly supported her bottom with his arm and placed his hand along her back.

Nyla couldn't help but blush at the sight of his large hands and long fingers as he held her daughter. Her body seemed to relive the luscious way he drove her mad with want by just using his fingers. Bringing her to some of the most intense orgasms she'd ever felt. She also couldn't stop staring at Andrew as he and her daughter had a very long staring match of their own.

Dee Dee suddenly cleared her throat, again. "Um, can I get you guys anything? Coffee?"

"Yes," Andrew answered without taking his eyes of the little girl that started babbling to him as if she was giving him a complete rundown of her life story.

Elese appeared next to Andrew smiling. Seeing as Andrew was uncharacteristically at a loss for words, she gave Dee Dee both hers and Andrew's coffee order.

"Your daughter is beautiful," Elese said to Nyla as she rubbed the little girl's back.

"Thank you," she replied still in awe of what was happening before her. Se'Nya was fickle when it came to strangers, especially men. So for her to go right to Andrew, without being prompted, told her a lot. Se'Nya evidently saw something in Andrew that she liked.

My baby has great taste, Nyla boasted silently.

Andrew smiled at Se'Nya but said to Nyla, "Nyla, this is a family friend of mine, Elese Michaels. Elese, this is Nyla Montgomery."

Elese smiled, her flawless skin revealing nothing but openness in her body language and her piercing, strong, green eyes as she stretched her hand out in greeting. "It's very nice to meet you, Nyla."

Nyla returned her smile, accepting Elese's hand, then recognized something she heard and asked, "Michaels? Why do I know…?"

Elese started nodding before Nyla could finish what she was saying. "Yes, John Michaels, Robert's attorney is my ex-husband."

Nyla's eyes grew and she looked to Andrew. "What's going on?"

Andrew shifted Se'Nya to his side so he could look at both Nyla and Elese.

"Elese practices family law, Nyla. She's actually the best in the business, almost better than I used to be when I practiced in that field."

Nyla looked up at him, eyebrows raised. "Really? I didn't know that. I mean, when I googled you, it only said that you practiced corporate law."

Andrew grinned. "You *googled* me?"

Nyla smiled and shook her head. "Yes, of course, I did. I wasn't sure what I was getting into, and I wanted to see if there was anything out there about you that I should know."

"Did I check out okay?"

"Well, not exactly. You're pegged as arrogant, cut-throat, and someone that would bring a poor elderly person down if it meant you would win your case."

Andrew looked at Nyla with a bemused smile plastered on his Adonis-like face. "Umph... All sounds like compliments to me. What did they say negative?"

Elese shook her head and looked at Nyla just as Dee Dee came with to-go cups.

The trio sat down at the nearest table. Nyla looked over at Darrius and was met with dark, egregious brown/black eyes. She knew how pissed he was, but for the life of her, she didn't understand why he stayed where he was. She just knew he would have stomped over to where they were, made his presence known, started shit with Andrew, and then left.

What Nyla didn't know was how much Darrius wanted to do just that. He hated to see this strange white motherfucka taunt him like he was doing. He wanted to kill him right in this diner but he found all the self-control he could muster not to move. He kept his mind on the bigger picture. There was more at stake here than his twisted need to kill so he remained where he was. Oh he kept the façade going, but deep down he knew things would eventually go his way. Besides, he knew he would get another chance to kill that fucker, and he couldn't wait.

"Ms. Montgomery... Can I call you Nyla?" Elese asked, giving Nyla a very assuring smile.

"Sure."

"Awesome, thank you. Nyla, Andrew has been consulting with me since he first took your case. He wants to make sure we have a solid case to keep Robert's grimy hands off this little girl."

Nyla shook her head. "I don't want him not to see Se'Nya. I just want to assure he won't run off with her, you know?" she scoffed and shook her head. "The bastard didn't even want me to have her. He tried to give me money to get rid of her. He said 'the others just took the money, Nyla. Don't be stupid.' I told him that I was doing no such thing, and he got mad and left, telling me that I was on my own."

Andrew's disdain for the man grew even more. As he looked down at this heavenly creature, he couldn't see how anyone would deny her.

"Yeah, that sounds like the little bastard. He can't handle anyone taking the attention off his spoiled ass. He thinks this world revolves around him and it doesn't," Elese announced.

Andrew's attention quickly moved from the three ladies at his table to Dee Dee and the dark-skinned man who had had his arm around Nyla. They were deep in conversation with the man throwing hostile looks at him.

"Who is the son of a bitch over there?" Andrew asked, making sure to raise his voice loud enough to be heard.

Nyla looked over at Darrius and knew things were going to be really bad once they spoke.

She sighed deeply. "Darrius is just a friend."

Andrew grunted and switched his attention back to the little one on his lap. He stood her up and held her hands as she bounced on his legs.

"I see more than just a simple friendship in his eyes," he added.

"Yeah, well, I didn't say it was simple," Nyla offered. "Darrius has been there for me, helping me with Se'Nya, giving me lifts every time my car breaks down. We've been friends for years."

"And you two were never a couple?" Elese asked.

"Nope, I just didn't think of him that way." Nyla looked back at Darrius and found his eyes were steady on her. Dee Dee caught her eye and shrugged her apology. Nyla sighed again and looked at Andrew. "Do you want to meet him? This might help this situation."

"That would not be a good idea," Andrew replied in a scathing tone.

"Why? What harm would it do?"

Andrew shook his head and grunted. "Baby, if I go over there, he might end up going through the window next to him. But if he continues to have that staring problem of his, he will no doubt still end up going through the window next to him."

Andrew looked over at Darrius, then smiled. "On second thought, maybe I should go and say hello."

"Uh no, you will not," Elese announced and stood. "Don't you have court to get back to?"

Andrew took one last glance at Darrius, then looked at Nyla. "I'm sorry for springing Elese on you without talking to you about it. It's just better for all parties if she took over the case."

Mind churning, Nyla asked, "Why? You don't want to help me anymore?"

"Sweetheart, that's not the case at all," Andrew told her, then looked to Elese.

Elese sat back down and touched Nyla's arm. "I told him that he needed to step down. It's a matter of conflict of interest." Nyla still looked questioningly at Elese, so she added, "Okay, think about how this caveman reacted when we walked in and he saw you with Darrius. Now times that by ten and that's what would happen if he represented you."

Andrew snorted. "It wouldn't be that bad."

"Ha, the hell it wouldn't."

Andrew grunted again and shifted his attention to Se'Nya.

Nyla studied him and realized what Elese said was undoubtedly true. She actually sensed it. She looked at Elese. "Okay, so what is your plan?"

"First, please know that you can trust me. Andrew and I have known each other since we were kids. Please have solace in knowing that if he trusts me with your case, then so can you." Elese let that resonate in the air for a second before she went on. "I'm very good at what I do, Nyla. I know my ex-husband like the back of my hand. Me being on this case assures that John will play this by the book. I know his secrets, the skeletons in his closet, everything. If he doesn't do this fair and by the book, he will pay dearly. Nyla, we are sending him a message; he can't win."

Nyla wanted to believe her; she really did. She just knew Robert wouldn't let this go easily. He was like a dog chewing on his favorite toy, and a person would lose their hand if they tried to separate that dog from his toy.

Andrew, feeling Nyla's hesitation, added, "Please don't misunderstand the intent here. I'll still be heavily involved in your case. The promise I made to you still stands. I'll just be doing it from the sidelines. I'll be the one keeping Robert honest; keeping him from playing dirty."

Nyla didn't hesitate. She nodded her head and told Elese. "Okay, I trust Andrew probably more than I should, but I do. So if he trusts you then so do I."

Andrew kissed Se'Nya on her cheek and reluctantly handed her over to Nyla. "I have to go, sweetheart. I have court in two hours. You are in good hands with Elese, and if there is anything that you have questions about, you have my number."

Andrew grabbed ahold of the back of Nyla's head, something that he was beginning to enjoy, and brought her closer to him. He kissed her a few times, fighting the urge to stick his tongue down her throat. He said to her, just above her lips, "Call me later tonight, whenever you get settled. I don't care how late it is. I just want to hear your voice."

Nyla smiled and replied softly, "I will."

He kissed her again and stood. He made eye contact with Darrius, waiting for the man to do or say something, but he didn't. Andrew then took a step as if he was heading in Darrius' direction. Nyla and Elese tensed and so did Darrius.

Andrew laughed.

Pussy.

Then he turned and left.

Elese leaned into her. "Girl, you have a lot on your hands with that one."

"Yeah, don't I know it." Nyla watched Andrew leave before she turned back to Elese. "I have to take Se'Nya to the doctors in a few, so please tell me how you're going to keep Se'Nya safe from the clutches of Robert."

* * *

Darrius stood by his car as he watched Nyla drive out of the diner's parking lot. They had managed to talk after the female lawyer left the diner and before Nyla had to leave for Se'Nya's doctor's appointment. Nyla slowly approached Darrius with bounds of apologies and proceeded to tell him everything she hadn't a few days ago. Darrius played his part and fussed about how she dismissed him like he wasn't shit, how she kissed some white fucker in front of him. She took a deep breath and finally told him about her feelings for the tall, blonde guy that he wanted nothing more but to rip to pieces. The control the man was supposed to have had disappeared quickly, and Darrius knew why. He had seen that type of rage before and it made him smile.

He pulled out his cell phone, searched for the number he needed and listened as the phone rang in his ear. When a voice picked up on the other end, he said into the phone.

"The cat may be out of the bag sooner than we wanted."

"It's too early," replied the person on the other end.

Darrius looked around the parking lot before he opened his car door and slid inside. "Yeah, I hear you, but she found him. Or rather he found her, but I don't think he actually knows what he's found."

The voice on the phone remained quiet for a second before Darrius heard, "Are you sure this is him?"

Darrius started his car. "Oh yeah, this is the one, I'm positive. He practically lost it in the diner where she worked because I had my arm around her. I could see it all over him. He wasn't thinking about anything but coming for me."

"Did he get close to you? Does he know who you are?"

"No. Are you not listening to what I'm telling you? This fucker was so enraged he wasn't thinking straight. He's that far gone over her."

The phone went silent for a few seconds, and Darrius waited.

He leaned back and closed his eyes. He came close to meeting his end at the hands of one of the strongest his generation had ever seen. There was no way he would've been able to survive the confrontation, not by himself anyway. He knew it, and as he remembered the look on Andrew's face, Andrew knew it too.

When this shit finally came to a head, Darrius hoped he would have the chance to wipe that smug look off of Andrew's face.

"Tell me about the man that you encountered," the voice on the phoned requested.

"I'll do better than that; I'll give you the bastard's name; Andrew Pierce."

"Shit!" the voice exclaimed quickly, and Darrius smiled.

"Yeah, this has surpassed our expectations. What do you want to do?"

"You will stick to the plans, making sure you're where you need to be in order to carry out your mission. We can't afford to screw this up."

"Yes, I know what I must do, but when I kill her, we have to be ready to act. We can't miss this opportunity. We will only have a small window for this plan to work. You have to get everyone ready."

"Don't you worry about everyone else. We were born ready for this. You just handle everything on your end and kill the girl, then take her daughter. We already have a family set up to take her in and raise her. If she's anything like her mother, we'll be ready."

Darrius snorted. "I can already tell you she is. Trust me on that."

The voice paused, but only for a second, before he said firmly, "Then kill the baby too. We can't take any more chances."

"I'll let you know when to get ready," Darrius said into his phone, before disconnecting the call.

He smiled again as he pulled out of the parking lot. Finally, he would be rid of this fucked up assignment and move on. He was tired of pretending to want this woman. He hated her with every fiber in his being. That's how he was taught, that's how he was raised. His grin grew as he thought about the moment when he would wrap his hands around Nyla's neck. To see the life fade from her eyes will be something he would never forget. Maybe he'd even fuck her before he killed her.

"Yeah, that sounds like a good plan."

TO BE CONTINUED ...

CONTROLLED 2: https://www.amazon.com/dp/B0767M4D4K

CONTROLLED 3: https://www.amazon.com/dp/B07B7F8G3N

Printed in Great Britain
by Amazon